Beautiful With You

Book Three of the Just Say Yes Series

Jen Andrews

Author's Note

This is the third and final book in the **Just Say Yes** series for characters Zoey and Andy.

This book contains sexual content, bad language, and physical violence between a man and a woman. This book is not appropriate for persons under the age of 18. Please read with caution.

Thank you.

~*Jen*

Dedication

For Lorrie, Kay, Jessica, Jen, Julie, and Jake.

I wouldn't be here without you cheering me on, and telling me daily to get off my lazy ass to get this book done.

I love you all!

Acknowledgements

I have so many people to thank I don't even know where to begin.

Lorrie Anson, I honestly don't know what I'd do without you. You have taught me so much and have been so patient with me, that I am surprised you haven't put a hit out on me. (Unless you did, and I just don't know about it yet.)

Kay Manis and Jessica Guerrero, you are my daily comic relief and I love you. Retirement is just around the corner (I wish) so get ready for the bus. I promise to keep the man candy on hand, at all times. It's now in writing, so you'd better hold me to it.

Jen Wildner, you are an awesome person and I can't believe you were crazy enough to say yes when I asked you to be my PA. Thank you for saying YES! #teamjen

To the ladies who beta read this book for me, thank you so much for your feedback and support! Anie "Butter" Michaels, Kendra Gaither, Danielle Bolme, and Jessica Guerrero.

To my Snowflakes: Thank you for all the pimping you do!

To my Kiwis: Jennie Coull and Sarah Underwood. Thank you for reading this book and making sure I had everything correct regarding New Zealand. Someday, I will make it back there and we'll get to meet in person and watch our AB's play some rugby.

This entire series, I have worked with two amazing artists who brought my books to life visually.

Thank you, Sarah, at Sprinkles on Top Studios, for designing my gorgeous covers.

Thank you, Tami, at Integrity Formatting, for the unique and creative formatting inside my books.

Both of you have put up with my ideas, changes, and creative input more times than I can count, and I appreciate you so much. I look forward to working with you both in the future on new books.

Thank you to all the bloggers who have shared, pimped, reviewed, and supported me! There are so many of you, it would take pages and pages to list you all. Just know that every blogger I have worked with, I appreciate you!

Last, but not least. To my IEZ girls, at The Indie Erogenous Zone. You are all talented authors, and I know who to turn to when I am having a bad day and need to vent. Twirl and flourish, ladies!

To everyone who has read the Just Say Yes series, THANK YOU.

If I forgot anyone, I am truly sorry!

~*Jen*

Foreword

It is said that when life gives you lemons, make lemonade.
Or when life knocks you down, get back up. When you fall
off the horse, get back on.

What do you do when life just keeps knocking you down,
repeatedly?

You get your ass up and *fight*.

~ Zoey

Chapter One

Zoey

August 2012

Monday morning came early for my friends and me. We went to sleep late after scheming all night to right the wrongs of one woman. The woman who had kept a baby from Andy—a baby who had died just hours after she was born. My fiancé's ex-wife was the woman in question.

That was if I still had a fiancé. He had left me. Did I mention I might be pregnant?

My life had been turned completely upside down, yet again.

The ex-wife, Michelle, had refused to speak to Andy about their baby, and he'd given up trying, so we were going to force her hand.

He'd also given up on us, and our future.

But I hadn't. And I wouldn't.

After everything I had been through, I was not going down without a fight. I'd worked too hard to get to where I was, just to let my life fall apart again. Sure, it was upside down for the time being, but I would get it right . . . Even if I had to do it on my own.

The first item on my agenda: To see a doctor.

After my friends left, I dialed my OB doctor's office only to find out I would have to wait until the following week for my appointment.

Sasha and Jess had tried to convince me all night that I needed to do a home pregnancy test, but I still refused. They didn't understand why I wouldn't do it, but I just *couldn't* take one. If the test were positive, I would stress myself out more because I would worry about genes and DNA. The scary thing was, I already knew what the test results would say. *How?* I just knew.

I'd been pregnant before and I knew all the signs. Unfortunately, they were the same as the side effects of my birth control, so I had been stupid and hadn't put two and two together. Plus, I didn't need the extra stress on top of what I was already dealing with; I didn't want to take a test to add to it.

Only I knew my stress limits, and I was extremely close to reaching that limit. I would simply take good care of myself, and accept the outcome when I had an official answer from my doctor.

Last night, I'd decided that Google was, once again, my friend, and I had found Michelle working at a very prominent real estate firm in San Francisco. And by prominent, I mean a high-rise portfolio and only catering to people with a shit ton of money. It was also owned by her family.

My friends and I had big plans to flush out "the bitch" and get her to talk, but first, I needed to make it through a week and a half of work. I needed to stay focused on the goal, and my goal was Andy. I loved him without question, but I was so angry with him.

It dawned on me sometime during our scheming session the previous night that he had taken my decisions away from me. He had decided that I needed to have kids of my own someday, without even talking to me about it. I was mad that he hadn't even considered adoption if we found out we couldn't have children together.

With my personal history of being in foster care and being adopted myself, I was more likely than anyone else to adopt a child. How could he overlook that? Why did he have to make such a rash decision and fucking leave me? I knew he was devastated by his loss, but we were supposed to stick by each other when times were tough, not just give up.

I was not a violent person, but right then, I felt the need to smack the living shit out of him. I wanted to yell and scream and make him listen to me, but no, he had left his freaking cell phone here, and I had no way to contact him.

He had taken my heart with him when he left and was probably half way back to New Zealand by now. The one thing that kept my hope alive was the possibility that there was a tiny part of him growing inside me.

It also scared me to death.

I decided to call his Aunt Sarah to see if she knew where he was and how he was doing. I had a few other questions, and she was the one person who might help me. With the hope that she would be willing to talk to me, I dialed her number.

"Hello, Maggie!" she chimed a little too merrily when she answered.

Huh?

"Hold on one moment please."

I heard the distinct click-clack noise of her high heels across the tile floor of her house. Sarah was going up the stairs and then I heard a door shut. "Zoey?" she said finally. "Sorry about that, I didn't want Hamish and A.J. to know it was you on the phone when I answered. I'm so glad you called. Are you okay?"

"I'm doing alright, I guess. Pretty angry really, if you want to know the truth."

She cleared her throat. "I can only imagine. I really don't know what A.J.'s thinking. It doesn't make any sense."

I agreed with her. "Is he still leaving?"

"Yes, he is. I'm so sorry," she said. "He's downstairs with Hamish packing boxes to ship to his house in New Zealand."

His house in New Zealand?

"What do you mean *his* house?" I asked. "How does he have a place to live already?"

"It's his parents' house, Zoey. He inherited everything, including the house, but his friend Tamati and his wife Iria have lived there since he came back to the States. They rent it from him and take care of it for him too. It works out well having someone he knows and trusts living there. I'm sorry, I thought you knew."

How nice. "No. I didn't. Apparently, he didn't think it was something he could share with me. I didn't know he owned a house."

My voice broke as I spoke, and I hated it, but I would deal with it later. I had information to gather first.

She started to say something else when there was a knock at her door. I clearly heard Andy ask Sarah if she knew where the packing tape was. I forced the tears back because I could hear the pain in his voice. He was not doing well.

"Yes A.J., just a minute," she called back to him. "Zoey, give me a second okay? Do you want me to see if he'll talk to you?"

"No, Sarah. Don't ask him, just hand him the phone. I don't care at this point if he wants to talk to me or not, I have something to say to him."

"Very well then," she said, her voice was terse. "Good luck."

I had a feeling she knew he was about to get an earful.

For the next few minutes, I heard muffled voices through the phone. I couldn't tell what Sarah and Andy were saying, but I could tell by the tone, the conversation was heated. He didn't want to talk to me and it broke my heart.

After a few seconds of silence, his voice came over the line.

"Zoey?"

Hot tears pricked my eyes when I heard his deep voice. I took in a few ragged breaths to calm my thundering heart. Suddenly, I didn't know what to say.

"Are you there?" he asked.

There was so much that I wanted to tell him, but I didn't know where to begin. I started rambling.

"I'm here. I've always been here, and I always will be. I don't know why you think it's okay for you to make decisions about my life for me."

He cleared his throat. "Zoey, please—" His voice was barely a whisper.

"No," I interrupted him. "You need to listen to me this time. How dare you? How fucking dare you think biological kids are a deal breaker for *us?* For me? Did you forget where I came from? Because I sure as hell didn't forget."

My voice cracked, and I couldn't stop myself from crying.

"Zoey, I'm so sorry. I didn't think—"

"No, you didn't. You didn't think about *me* at all did you? You gave up on us. Were we not worth fighting for?"

He took a breath to speak, but again, I didn't let him.

"Don't answer that question. While you're running away and avoiding this entire situation, you need to know I'm going to fight for us. Don't you dare think this is over, because it's not. Not by a long shot. So go to New Zealand, and do whatever it is you need to do, and just remember your family is here missing you and that you are acting like a coward."

He exhaled, his voice faltering as he spoke. "I am a coward. You should hate me."

I was still so angry, but I knew his heart was broken far worse than mine was.

"Andy, I could never hate you. I will only ever love you. There are things going on here you know nothing about . . . go ahead and take the easy way out, and get on that plane. You let me get on a plane months ago to deal with my shit and that is the *only* reason I am not putting up a fight about you leaving. But while you're there, you need to remember that I am still here, wearing my beautiful engagement ring, and I don't intend to take it off. Can you put Sarah back on the phone now, please? I've said everything I need to say."

Inside, I felt horrible for saying all of that to him, because I never wanted to hurt him, but I needed to make one last attempt to get through—to make him see that he didn't need to leave me, and that things would work out.

"Alright, I'm handing the phone back to her."

"Andy, wait!" I cried.

"Yeah, Beautiful?" he said softly.

He was clearly feeling the weight of the situation on his shoulders and the thought crossed my mind that it might be the very last time I would ever hear him call me that. I could hardly speak as tears rolled down my face and my voice wavered with raw emotion.

"There's one more thing I need to say. I love you, don't ever forget it."

"Never," he whispered.

Sarah came back on the line. "I don't know what you said to him, but I think you got his attention."

It made me feel a bit better, but I knew he would still leave. "Good. He needed to hear everything I said to him."

On a mission, I picked up Andy's cell phone off my dresser and began scrolling through his contacts.

"Zoey? Did you call me for a reason or were you calling for A.J.?"

"Yes, I'm sorry. I have some questions, but a couple of them have already been answered. Now I know where Andy's going and who he's staying with."

Not wasting any time, I found Tamati and Iria's phone numbers in his cell. "Can you give me his address in New Zealand, please? I want to mail his birthday present to him."

I grabbed a pen and paper and scribbled the address down then repeated it back to her to double-check it. "Thank you Sarah, I appreciate your help."

After our call was over, I added Tamati and Iria's phone numbers to my cell, then connected both mine and Andy's phones to my laptop and transferred all the pictures from them. Once the photos were transferred, I copied all the photos of us together to a thumb drive. Originally, I was going to get him something different for his birthday, but I needed to be sure he wouldn't forget what we had together. I hoped the photos would remind him.

I wasn't expecting to talk to Andy when I'd called Sarah, so our conversation threw me off balance. Yet because of it, I was even more determined than before to get him back. I would still give him the time he needed to sort himself out, as he had for me. I owed him that much.

Unfortunately, I had to go to work, and later, I had a birthday present to make. I headed to the store first to make sure everything was going well. The morning was moving right along for a Monday, so I went into the office and ordered a few parts and general stock items that we needed.

Once I was finished at the store, I headed next door to the shop. I refused to look over to where his truck and trailer were usually parked. I stopped dead in my tracks when I walked into the mechanic bays and saw Andy's rolling toolbox was gone. It hurt like hell to see it was no longer there. Every trace of him had vanished, and I choked back a sob at the sight.

Noah looked up from the car he was working on in the next bay and stopped what he was doing. He picked up a rag and wiped his hands off as he came over to me.

"Hey Z," he said apprehensively. "Jess told me what was going on. I'm sorry about everything. He really left, huh?"

I nodded, trying not to let my emotions get the best of me. Damn it, I was a fighter and I was not going to lie down and give up this time.

"She told me about your plan. You let me know if you need anything, or if you need someone with some muscle to help, okay?"

"I will Noah. Thank you." I hugged him and glanced over at the rest of my brothers who were watching our exchange.

Within the next minute, my four brothers had surrounded me. None of them said a word. After a silent, group hug, we went our separate ways.

Since the staff had everything covered at work, I left early to go to a camera store that sold everything you could possibly ever need for photography and photo projects. I gave the clerk my thumb drive so he could print all the photos on it for me.

I had an eight by ten enlargement made of a photo of Andy and me from Jess and Noah's wedding. Memories from that night flooded my mind as I wandered around the store. He looked so handsome in his tux, and we had sung together for the first and only time, for Jess and Noah's first dance as a married couple.

He had almost proposed to me that day, but my big mouth got in the way. Oh God, if I'd only kept my mouth shut. We might not have gone to Sonoma that weekend and run in to Corey. None of this would be happening.

I was having a hard time not placing the blame on myself for him leaving. It wasn't my fault, but if he had proposed to me back in June, who knew what would have happened in the meantime.

Coulda, shoulda, woulda, Zoey. You can't dwell on it. It is what it is, and you need to fix it.

While the photos were printing, I picked out a frame for the enlargement, a nice photo album, and a packet of colored postcards with decorative borders that would fit in with the pictures I planned to put in the photo album.

Once I left the shop, prints and supplies in hand, I took myself out to lunch. As I picked at my food and looked through the photos, I jotted down a list of songs that were special to us.

At home, later that evening, I arranged the photos in the album by date, leaving one slot empty on each page. Then, on the postcards, I printed the lyrics that related best to each group of photos.

On the last page, were the photos taken just minutes after Andy proposed. My favorite photo, the one we had sent to everyone in a text announcing our engagement, was placed next to a postcard with my handwritten note:

> To be continued . . . I purposely left this album unfinished, because we are not finished. There will be many more memories to come. This is my promise to you. We will fill countless albums in our lifetime. Albums full of us, our children, and someday, our grandchildren. We only live one life, Andy. I chose to live mine with you the day you asked me to say yes . . . I will always say yes to you. I need you to say yes to me this time. Please don't give up on us. I love you.
>
> Zoey

I wrapped the album with the same elegant, black wrapping paper and silver ribbon I'd wrapped his Valentine's Day present in months ago then shipped the gift to him in New Zealand.

It would arrive on his birthday, the same day as my doctor's appointment.

Chapter Two

Andy

She was right. Zoey was spot on when she called me a coward. How could I have done something so fucking cruel to the person who had brought me back to life?

Before her, I was a shell of the person I once was. Granted, I put on a brave front, but inside, I was still broken. Prior to the accident that killed my family, I was happy. Never wanted for anything, had everything going for me, and because of my cocky attitude from being the top rugby player at school, I had cost them their lives. One instance of retaliation against another player was the reason my family was dead.

I thought I'd moved past blaming myself for their deaths, but apparently, I hadn't. Again, I was suffering from guilt and held myself responsible for another death.

Zoey and I had worked through the issues between us while she was on vacation months ago. And afterwards, we'd continued to flourish as a couple every day. I never wanted to spend a day without her for the rest of my life. Yet, here I sat, leaning my back against the willow tree where I'd proposed to her just days ago, thinking about what had changed since then.

Emma.

Stinging tears pricked my eyes at just the thought of her name. How could I have had a daughter and not known? Why hadn't Michelle told me? What a fucking cruel twist of fate that brought my seemingly perfect world crashing down around me.

Emma.

What a sweet name for a little girl who would never call me "Daddy." A little girl I never saw or knew about until it was far too late. God, what I would have done to see her, to have held her in my arms. Did she look like me? What color were her eyes and hair? How long did she live? Would I ever get to see her? In a picture? After I died? Did she suffer, or go peacefully in her sleep?

All questions that held no answers.

Fuck. What did it matter? She was gone and there wasn't a damn thing I could do about it. It mattered because she was *mine*. A part of me, part of my parents and sister. A part of *us* I could never get back.

Being Kiwi, and in our culture, family was the most important part of your life and you took care of them.

I had failed.

Miserably.

At being a son, brother, husband, fiancé, and apparently, a father. I had also failed Zoey in the worst possible way. By leaving her. When she'd called Aunt Sarah earlier that day and I spoke with her, she'd asked me if I'd forgotten where she came from. The truth was, I had been so caught up in my own grief from finding out about

Emma, and then leaving her, that I *had* forgotten about her adoption.

Her adoptive family took me in as if I was one of their own over the months Zoey and I had been together. Just the way they had when they adopted her. It was like she'd always been a part of them. Not the daughter of a drug addicted mother and an absentee father. She was a James, through and through. And under the tree where I now sat completely destroyed, I had asked her to be my wife, to take my last name.

Later that night, she'd asked me to give her until after we were married to talk seriously about having kids. When those words spilled from her perfect pink lips, my heart thumped so hard in my chest it resonated in my ears and I could barely hear my response to her. She'd said yes to me. She'd said yes to children, just not so soon, but she'd still said yes. I could see it in her eyes, and if I knew Zoey, she wanted children as badly as I did to make up for her horrible childhood and to give me a family. She would have done anything for me, and I, her.

Sadly, none of that would ever happen—because I was a coward. I was scared that something was wrong with me, and I would pass it down to our kids. And since Michelle refused to speak with me, there was no way to know if I was the cause of yet another death. I couldn't do that to Zoey. She'd already lost one child and I couldn't let her lose another. She would be better off without me.

Even on the night of Jess and Noah's wedding, when I'd confessed to her that I was ready for my own family, I could see the hope and love in her eyes when I told her that she was the only one I wanted to have that family with. I knew she hadn't been ready—she knew, too. But, I'd had to tell her how I felt, and I knew in my heart it was something she would want when the time was right for her.

The sound of an ATV pulling into the clearing interrupted my thoughts of the future I would never have.

Hamish stopped the ATV near the willow tree and shut off the motor.

"It's time to go, son. We need to get on our way to the airport."

Without saying a word, I stood and walked in a daze to the ATV and took my seat next to Hamish.

"Are you sure this is what you want to do A.J?" he asked after pulling into the garage at the house.

No, it wasn't what I wanted at all. But what else could I do? Marrying Zoey and having a family with her was what I wanted, but now I knew about Emma. Leaving the States was the only way I could guarantee that I would stay away from Zoey and let her move on—to live the life she deserved. My heart ached at the thought I'd broken hers.

"Hamish, I don't have a choice," I said. "Zoey deserves to have everything that I can't give her."

"Son, you're being unreasonable."

I raised my hand to keep him from going further. "Stop, I'm not your son. My father is dead because of me," I muttered then got out of the ATV.

At the San Francisco airport, Hamish dropped me off at the curb like I had asked him to because I didn't want to deal with any difficult goodbyes to him and Sarah.

I stepped up to the ticket counter.

The man behind the counter asked, "How may I help you, sir?"

At that moment, I froze. My mouth wouldn't open and I just stared at the man. The hand that held my passport and I.D. automatically set them down and pushed them toward him.

"Auckland," I finally managed to say. "One way, please, on the next flight." I didn't have a plan other than to get back to En Zed as quickly as possible.

"Yes, sir." He picked up my I.D. and passport, then quickly typed on his keyboard. "I'm afraid our coach seating is all booked up until tomorrow. The only seats available on the next flight are first class." He glanced from the screen to meet my eyes. "That flight leaves in two hours, but is very expensive. Did you want me to get you booked on one of the flights tomorrow?"

I pulled out my wallet, dug behind the cards I frequently used and slipped out the black credit card that I'd never used. "No, I'll take the first class flight tonight, please. I don't care what the cost is."

What good was having the money if I wasn't going to use it? I handed the card to him.

He looked at it, then back at me. Without asking a question, or telling me the price, he booked me on a first class, one-way flight back to Auckland.

The flight was comfortable enough, but I was so miserable I couldn't eat or sleep. Fortunately, I had a seat with nobody close by to bother me. By the time we landed in Auckland, I was an emotional mess. One part of me wanted to go straight over to the ticket counter and buy a ticket back to Zoey, and the other part just wanted to disappear.

When the taxi pulled up in front of the gates at my house, I paid the driver and exited the car. That's when I realized I didn't have a key to get inside. Iria's car was still there so she hadn't left for work yet, or had the day off. I knocked on my own front door, and a few minutes later, it swung open to reveal my best mate's very surprised wife.

Her eyes widened and her mouth dropped open at the sight of me.

"A.J.? What are you doing here?"

Taking in a deep breath, I said the only thing I could. "I fucked up."

I was petrified when the day finally came for my doctor's appointment so I asked my mom to go with me. When we arrived, the receptionist sent me straight to the lab where they drew some blood and had me pee in a cup.

Afterward, I sat with my mom in the waiting room and fidgeted like crazy until she reached out and rubbed my back to help me relax.

"Zoey, calm down, everything will be fine."

I sure hoped she was right.

Finally, the nurse called me back. We stopped at the scale to get my weight. I had gained five pounds since the last time I weighed myself. I was one hundred percent certain I'd gained it all in my stomach, because I had a hard time buttoning my shorts that morning. The same pair of shorts, which had been a bit loose the last time I wore them.

After she took my blood pressure and made notes in my chart, the nurse led me into an office and asked me to sit in a chair, in front of the doctor's desk. Oh my God. That freaked me out.

She must have noticed. "Do you want me to get your mom, Zoey?" She smiled, kind of like she knew a big secret.

Even though I had already semi-convinced myself of it, I knew right then I was pregnant. I still didn't understand how it could have happened though.

Holy fucking shit. I nodded and swallowed hard so I wouldn't throw up.

She left the room and when my mom arrived she asked, "*Mija,* what's going on?"

Shaking my head in disbelief, I swallowed again and opened my mouth to speak right as my doctor came in.

"Good morning, Zoey, how are you?" Dr. Stewart sat at her desk and flipped open my chart.

"I will be doing better once you tell me what's going on," I replied as the butterflies fluttered around my stomach.

She scanned the papers in front of her for a few seconds and then looked me in the eyes. "Well," she said, as she looked down at the paper in front of her again. "According to this, you're pregnant."

I sucked in a deep breath, held it, then slowly let it out as I squeezed my mom's hand. I glanced over at her, and she was smiling, her eyes sparkling with unshed tears.

"I don't understand how this could happen, Dr. Stewart. I've been on the pill for years. I've wracked my mind and I *know* I haven't missed any." *Jesus, I counted the fuckers ten times just to be sure!*

She smiled. "The results don't lie, Zoey. Why don't we go into an exam room and do an ultrasound to see how far along you are. That should tell us more and maybe something will jog your memory."

So many thoughts and emotions flooded through not only my head, but also my entire body while I was alone in the room changing. Pregnant . . . how? In a daze, I perched on the edge of the exam table.

When the doctor and my mom came in, Dr. Stewart asked, "When was the first day of your last period?"

I pulled my tiny day planner out of my purse. I was nothing, if not organized. I already knew my last period had been in May, but I wasn't sure of the exact date so I flipped through my calendar.

"It was May twenty-second. I switched from the monthly pack to the three-month pill pack then, so I haven't had my period since."

She nodded and made notes in my chart. "You've already said you didn't miss any pills. Were you sick or did you have any illnesses where you needed to take antibiotics? They are the most common reason your birth control might fail."

I shook my head. I hadn't taken any antibiotics in well over a year, and hadn't taken any medicine other than ibuprofen for headaches and the pain pills after my accident. But, that was months ago.

"Let's see what we have going on in here then, Zoey." She smiled. "Once we can see how far along you are, we should know more."

She lifted the gown and squirted gel on my lower belly.

"Well, it seems you are already starting to show," she said, surprised after she saw my stomach. She pressed the wand against me and slid it back and forth through the gel. Dr. Stewart held it still when she had the image she wanted on the screen. She let out a soft laugh. "Let's get some measurements here. You are definitely further along than I anticipated."

What the hell?

Dr. Stewart pointed to our baby on the screen and showed Mom and I the tiny head and body. She pressed a few buttons on the machine as she moved the wand around. My brain tried to comprehend everything that was happening as I stared at the screen in disbelief. Andy should have been right there with me to see the life we'd created, but he wasn't.

Just as the tears formed in my eyes, my mom stood from her chair and wrapped me in her arms, pulling my cheek against her chest. "Baby girl, I know you're scared and heartbroken, but you're so strong now. You can do this. I have no doubt in my mind about that. You're going to be a wonderful mama," she whispered into my ear.

Hoping she was right, I nodded because I was temporarily rendered speechless. After I wiped away the tears that had escaped, Mom returned to her chair and we focused on the screen again.

"Does everything look normal, Dr. Stewart?" I paused as notions of Andy's concerns invaded my thoughts. He had previously mentioned DNA and possible issues with his genes causing Emma's death and I was scared he could be right.

She smiled, reassuring me. "Yes, everything looks perfectly normal. It seems you're around fourteen weeks based on the measurements I've taken."

Fourteen weeks? Holy fucking shit!

Chapter Three

Zoey

Fourteen weeks? How was it even remotely possible that I was already through my first trimester? Of course, I'd had suspicions that I might be pregnant, but fourteen weeks along?

I felt like a moron because I'd seen too many episodes of that television show about people who didn't know they were pregnant until they went in to labor. I had obviously misinterpreted several indications from my body.

However, it did explain several incidents that had happened over the last few months. Gagging on my toothbrush, which my mom said happened to her constantly when she was pregnant with Adam, being nauseous, which I just assumed was stress related, feeling dizzy when I moved, on occasion. The extra eating, the increased emotions . . . oh and the tiredness. Every damn day.

Doctor Stewart put the wand away and scooted her rolling stool closer to me, leaving the paused sonogram of our sweet child on the screen. Unable to take my eyes off the machine, I stared in awe at our tiny baby.

I was going to be a mom. Part of Andy and me was growing inside of my body.

At that very second, I knew I'd never been happier in my life. With or without Andy, I wanted and loved that child more than my own life.

"Alright Zoey, it's time to put your thinking cap on now," she said as she tapped away on the keyboard of her laptop. "You would've had to conceive around June fifth. What did you have going on in your life around that time?"

I stifled a giggle. I was *obviously* having sex around that time. Jesus, when was I not having sex since that day in Cabo back in February? It was practically a daily occurrence and the reason I'd switched birth control pills.

I flipped my calendar to June. I hadn't marked anything down for June fifth, but there was something for June sixth. *Drag races with Andy.*

Oh, holy shit . . .

An extremely surprised and shrill laugh erupted from me when I realized I'd gotten knocked up on the hood of Andy's car during our little tryst in his car trailer.

My mom and doctor stared at me with their eyebrows raised, waiting for me to say something.

Why did the birth control pill fail though? I thought back to Dr. Stewart's previous question about being sick, and then it dawned on me . . . I had been sick with the flu the week before the drag races, but I hadn't taken any antibiotics.

Could just being sick cause my birth control to fail?

"I think I remembered something," I said.

"What is it, Zoey?" Dr. Stewart asked.

Well, I definitely wasn't going to share the great sex on the car story. "I was really sick with the flu the week before I would have conceived. I threw up for four days straight and actually lost a lot of weight because of it."

"Sure, I guess that's possible, Zoey. If you were within the first week or so of your new pill pack and couldn't keep anything down, it was probably not in your stomach long enough to get into your system and you ovulated."

Thoughts of Emma passed through my mind suddenly. I was scared and had questions I hoped the doctor could answer. I would accept the information she gave me, and deal with it in whatever way I had to.

"Dr. Stewart, are there any noninvasive tests you can do to check for gene or DNA issues?"

"Is there something in particular you're concerned about?"

I gave her a brief description of what little we'd learned about Emma.

"Without knowing exactly what was wrong with that baby, we really won't know what to test for," she said. "We can run the standard tests of course, but if you can find out what caused the baby's death, we can do more specific tests."

"Do you want to hear your baby's heartbeat now?" she asked.

I nodded. "Yes, please. I'd love nothing more." A minute later, the whooshing sound of our baby's heartbeat filled the room. The three of us sat for a few minutes as we watched the baby twitch around inside me.

I thought to myself how much I wished Andy were here with me to see his child on the screen. I thought of how much he had missed with Emma. Before I knew it, my mom was handing me a Kleenex because I was crying.

Dr. Stewart printed out a couple of pictures for me to take home. I told her that as soon as I could find out about Emma, I would let her know.

Once I was alone in the room, I let myself cry for the baby growing inside me, for Andy, and for myself. I prayed I had the strength for everything that was about to happen. After getting dressed, I sent a text to Jess, Sasha, Will and Justin.

It's official . . . Fourteen weeks along. Time to get the rest of our plans underway.

When I exited the exam room, I collected the prenatal vitamins, a DVD of my sonogram from the receptionist, and scheduled my next appointment.

I wanted to tell Andy so badly, but for his sake, I needed the confirmation that our baby was healthy. I hated keeping it from him, but really didn't see any other alternative until I had more information.

Right then, I felt like the world's biggest hypocrite.

I was so angry at what Michelle had done by keeping Emma from him, yet here I was doing the exact same thing. The situation was completely different, because I intended to tell Andy as soon as possible, regardless of whether our baby was healthy or not.

The pregnancy was completely unexpected and unplanned, but when I saw our baby on the screen, I knew without a doubt, I loved the tiny life growing inside me. I hoped Andy would be thrilled about it, and I decided right then my mission was to find out what I could about Emma first to spare him any more pain.

The look on Andy's face when Corey told him about Emma was something I never wanted to see again. He had been completely blindsided, yet again. I'd never seen a man more broken in my life. It was as if his entire world had been yanked right out from under him.

Because it had been. It was up to me to put his world back in place in regards to Emma, and try to keep myself together at the same time. He had given up hope, but I couldn't. There was too much at stake.

After my doctor's appointment, Mom and I sat down at a restaurant for lunch and I called my dad.

"Baby girl, how was the appointment?" he asked without saying hello.

My dad was not Andy's biggest fan right then. I didn't blame him for being mad at him for leaving. I was mad at him too.

My mouth opened to speak, but the words wouldn't come out. I was worried my dad was going to be even angrier once he found out I was pregnant. The fact that my birth mother neglected and abandoned me never sat right with him. He didn't understand how someone could leave their child. Now, not only had Andy left me, but he'd unknowingly left our baby too.

"Zoey, are you still there?"

After clearing my throat, I mumbled, "Yeah, I'm still here."

He waited patiently on the other end of the line for me to tell him about how my appointment went.

"I'm fourteen weeks pregnant," I said quickly. "Dad, before you can get any angrier, you need to know what happened. My pill failed because I was sick with the flu. He never would have left if he'd known . . ."

He exhaled. "Zoey, come by for dinner tonight so we can talk in person, please."

Shit. This is not good. He sounded upset.

"Okay, but Dad, please don't be mad at me. I know you're not happy with him right now, but *I* need your support," I said with a shaky voice. I didn't want to disappoint my dad, ever.

"*Mija,* let me talk to him," my mom said when she realized the conversation was not going well.

Without warning my dad, I handed her the phone, and she began talking to him in Spanish. Crap. I hated it when they did that. I was the only one in the family who didn't speak Spanish.

They tried to teach me after I was adopted, but it would not click in my brain. I could understand for the most part, what people were saying, but to put responses together correctly and say the words properly . . . Yeah, I could not grasp it and constantly said words backward or out of order.

Plus, I couldn't roll my R's to save my ass.

I tuned my mom out because I didn't want to listen to her argue with my dad because of me. I knew enough Spanish to know she was not happy with him.

She hung up with my dad a few minutes later, and I waited for her to take a drink of her water.

"Is he mad at me?" I asked hesitantly.

"No Zoey. He's not mad at *you.*"

Great.

Good for me . . . bad for Andy.

"You know how he feels about our Andy leaving."

Yeah, I sure did. Our food arrived, and I dug in because of course, I was starving. I heard my mom snicker, so I looked up at her.

"Slow down *Mija,* you'll make yourself sick."

I set my fork down, wiped my mouth with my napkin, and chewed slowly. "Is this better?" I asked with a mouthful of food, just because I knew it grossed her out when people talked with food in their mouths. My brothers loved a good game of "See Food" during family dinner on occasion, and for some reason I felt the need to play right then even though my brothers weren't here.

"You're just like your disgusting brothers sometimes." She shook her head, laughed, and then started on her own lunch.

After a minute, she set her silverware down and turned to me. "Zoey, give your dad a few days to adjust to the news, please. He'll get over it."

"Of course I will, Mom." I nodded.

He needed a few days, and I *definitely* needed a few days to process the news. I could deal with that.

When we finished lunch, my mom insisted on going to a maternity clothing store, since she pointed out to me that I was about to bust the button off my shorts. I didn't want to be one of those women who looked frumpy, or wore their regular clothing during their pregnancies even though it was four sizes too small.

I ended up trying on, and liking several sundresses I could grow in to over the next couple of months while the weather was still warm. I'd practically been living in sundresses anyway. I might get as big as a beached whale, but I still wanted to look and feel pretty. Not to mention be comfortable.

While I was in the fitting room, my phone blew up with texts from my friends and family giving their congratulations and support. I desperately needed to take a moment to myself, so I sat on the bench in the fitting room.

An uncontrollable wave of guilt came over me because I wasn't going to tell Andy until the time was right.

He should have been the first person to know.

I just wanted him to come back to me. I couldn't breathe without him. My phone pinged with another text. It was from Sasha, and it simply read,

September 6th, 1 pm.

My heart thumped in anticipation. Our plan was coming together, slowly, but surely. My friend was going to be on the frontlines, while I waited patiently on the sidelines. That was our agreement since my pregnancy had been confirmed. She was, under no circumstances, allowing me on the frontline of the fight.

Sasha was going to meet with Michelle under the guise of a spoiled rich princess, who was looking for a nice high-rise apartment for her "daddy" to buy her.

Sasha was really playing the part well too. She had washed out the purple and black dye and dyed her hair to its natural color. We finally knew what color her hair was supposed to be—platinum blonde! She even borrowed a few high dollar outfits from one of her friends. She was ready to get her "rich bitch" attitude on.

I was definitely going to San Francisco, just in case, but I wasn't sure if I would attend the meeting with her or not, but I desperately wanted to. We weren't sure if Michelle knew who I was, or if her brother had even mentioned speaking to Andy.

While I was in the fitting room, my mom kept hanging more clothes over the door for me to try on. I bought enough clothes to last me a few more months while my baby belly grew. We headed back to my apartment, unloaded all of my shopping bags, and took them upstairs.

As soon as my mom left to go back over to the shop, I went to the kitchen to take the first of my prenatal vitamins. The message light was blinking on my answering machine. I pressed the play button and the room was flooded with Andy's deep voice.

"Hey, Beautiful . . . I just wanted to call and say thank you for the photo book. It means so much that you made it for me, and thought of me on my birthday. I didn't get the chance to tell you when we talked last time, but . . . I love you, Zoey. So much. I know I've fucked things up . . . And I'm so sorry. Please know that I love you. I'll talk to you soon."

I swore in the time he'd been back in New Zealand his accent had gone completely native. He sounded like he never left there. I listened to his message one more time, just to hear his voice.

He said he would talk to me soon. He didn't mention the postcard where I'd practically begged him not to give up on us.

Please, I needed him to be optimistic. *For us.* I just needed more time.

Chapter Four

Zoey

Since I was worn out, I decided to take a nap before I headed to my parents for dinner and to talk to my dad. In my bedroom, I pulled Andy's dresser drawer open out of habit and found that he had left me his New Zealand T-shirt. It was the only thing in the drawer.

Quickly, I stripped off my clothes and pulled his shirt over my head. With his scent surrounding me, I crawled onto his side of the bed, resting my head on his pillow that smelled of him.

I fell asleep quickly. Later, I awoke to my phone ringing. I scrambled across the bed to answer it, hoping it was Andy.

"Hello," I murmured, still half asleep.

"Oh *Mija,* sorry. Did I wake you?"

I glanced over at the clock on the nightstand to see what time it was—dinnertime. "Yeah Mom, I'm sorry. I fell asleep. I'm on my way over now."

"Alright, we were starting to get worried about you," she said.

We ended our call and I pulled on some stretchy yoga pants, and flip-flops. So much for my not-looking-frumpy-while-pregnant idea I'd had earlier.

After dinner, my dad and I sat down in the living room to talk.

"Zoey," he said. "I'm sorry for being a jerk earlier when you called. I should have been more supportive."

I shook my head, took in a deep breath, and let it out slowly. "I understand why you're upset. I'm upset with him too. I'm trying to understand everything from Andy's point of view. We haven't dealt with the things he has in his life. He has his aunt and uncle left, but that's it. If you had seen the look on his face when he was told he had a baby, and she was *dead* . . . it was horrible. He doesn't deal with death well."

Well shit, who does? But to be the sole survivor of a crash that killed your entire family . . . that would be excruciating for anyone to deal with.

A light bulb blinked on in my head, and I realized then, maybe he hadn't really dealt with it. I thought back to the few conversations we actually had about the accident and his move to the USA.

Hamish and Sarah had plucked him right out of his life and moved him thousands of miles from everything he'd ever known. Everything he'd ever loved. He needed New Zealand for comfort, to be close to the family he loved and had lost. Even though they were no longer alive, he still needed them.

Maybe going home to New Zealand was his way of dealing with Emma's death. It's not like he would get any type of closure from Michelle. I just wished he had chosen to need me instead of New Zealand. I was real and could help him.

Ugh, I hated thinking about it. Not knowing what he was feeling and thinking didn't help, and since he had shut me out, I would just have to wait until I talked to him. The letter he had written me explained his reasons for leaving me, but there had to be more to it.

My dad took a drink from his coffee mug then set it back on the table. Patting his thighs, he motioned for me to sit on his lap like I was a small child.

I didn't hesitate; I needed my dad's support more than anything. He was, once again, the main man in my life, so I scrambled onto his lap.

"I'm sorry, honey. Your mom set me straight after she came home and I've been thinking about everything since we talked this morning."

I hugged his neck and kissed his cheek. "Thanks Dad. I hope everything is fine with this baby. That is my main priority right now, even over Andy."

"Speaking of that baby," he said with a smile. "Let's see that tummy. I heard it's already starting to poke out there."

Giggling, I stood from his lap and pulled up the hem of my shirt a bit, and the top of my yoga pants down to rest right under the slight roundness of my abdomen.

"Oh Zoey, I swear it wasn't there last week when you were here," he said as he placed his hands on my stomach.

"I know!" I was just as surprised as he was. "It wasn't there one day, and the next, *poof*. There it is."

His hands still resting on me, my dad scooted forward on the couch and leaned in closer.

"Hey in there, little baby," he said in a low, soothing tone. "It's your grandpa. We're so excited to have you here, and I can't wait to meet you. You're going to be so beautiful like your mama, or handsome like your dad."

Tears stung my eyes and I held my breath for a minute so I wouldn't cry. "Thank you, Daddy," I whispered as the tears rolled down my cheeks. So much for not crying.

I hadn't called him "daddy" in ages. Memories from years before came flooding back to me. I had never had a dad until him. As a little girl, I always dreamed of being a daddy's girl, like some of the girls in my class had been.

I wanted a big, strong dad to rescue me from my mom's neglect. Someone to pick me up and swing me around until we were both so dizzy we fell down laughing.

Someone to show me how to be a *kid*. A dad to read me stories at bedtime, and tuck me in at night.

I confessed this to him shortly after I was adopted, and that very night, even though I was fourteen years old, he came into my room at bedtime and read me a story.

He had read to me every night for a year, and I loved him for it. He read all of the books nobody had read to me as a child. I didn't care that at my age, he was reading me Snow White, Cinderella, and The Pokey Little Puppy. I had *needed* it. The bond that I had formed with my dad was unbreakable.

I hoped our baby would have the same bond with Andy.

We hugged until my mom came in and joined us. "I hate to break this up," she said quietly as she touched each of our shoulders. "But dessert is ready."

My dad and I looked at each other and smiled. "Race ya!" I joked as we broke apart then sprinted to the kitchen. I had a feeling he let me win.

The day that Sasha was to meet with Michelle was quickly approaching. Since we were swamped at the shop and the store, I was constantly going back and forth between the two businesses. After work, I ran around like a chicken with its head cut off visiting friends and family because I didn't want to be home alone. I even made a few appointments to talk with Dr. Jensen even though I hadn't needed to talk to her in quite some time.

Each day, I found myself taking a few minutes of time to sit alone and think about Andy and our baby. Most of the time, I ended up crying from missing him and keeping the news of our baby from him.

I also realized that I needed to take each day one at a time, and not let myself fall back to my old ways. It would not be healthy for our baby or me. I had a plan, and I needed to follow through with it, keeping as much of my sanity intact as possible. But, I also knew that I needed to face the loss of Andy in my life until I could get him back.

The day before we were to drive to San Francisco for our meeting, I decided to stay home from work for the morning to pack a bag for my trip, and finish a few last minute chores around the apartment.

When my cell phone rang around noon, I knew by the ring tone that it was Noah.

"Hey, Noah."

"Hey, baby sis, you busy?" He sounded anxious.

"No, just stepped out of the shower, what's up?"

"You need to get over here to the shop right now," he said, trying to keep his voice down. "There's a woman over here asking for Andy."

"I'm on my way."

I threw my towel onto the bed and pulled a sundress over my head as I shoved my feet into the nearest shoes I could find. I ran a brush through my hair as quickly as I could and made it to the shop in less than five minutes.

As I entered the shop, Noah was coming down the hallway.

"Zoey, she took off," he said, obviously annoyed. "I'm sorry, I tried to stall her."

Shit! "It's okay. It's not your fault. Did she tell you her name?"

He shook his head.

Double shit! "What did she look like?"

"Shorter than you, mid-twenties I guess, dark hair." He closed his eyes in concentration. "She was really dressed up—though. She had one of those big manila envelopes with her." He opened his eyes again. "Sorry Z, I tried to stop her from leaving. I asked her to sit in the office to wait because we had customers in the lounge. When I came back in from calling you, she was practically running out the front door. She was mumbling something, but I couldn't understand her."

Maybe she left the envelope on the desk. I hurried past Noah and into the office. There was nothing out of place and no manila envelope.

Crap. Who was it? Based on the description Noah gave, she sounded like a businesswoman, maybe a lawyer? Maybe his ex-wife? But why would she be in Sacramento if she wouldn't talk to him before?

"Z, I'm so sorry," Noah said from the doorway. "I left her alone in the office to call you. I should have stayed with her so she wouldn't leave."

I patted him on the shoulder. "It's fine, Noah. You did what you could. If she comes back, she comes back. If not, then it wasn't meant to be."

We both left the office, Noah heading back to work and me heading back home to finish getting ready for the day. When I arrived home, the message light on my answering machine was blinking. Again, the message was from Andy.

"Hey there, Beautiful. I couldn't sleep, and just wanted to call and hear your voice. Hope you're doing well . . . I love you."

That was the second time I had missed his call. He said he couldn't sleep. Not having any idea what time it was in New Zealand, I found an app on my phone and converted the time between here and New Zealand. It was just after seven a.m. in Auckland when he had called.

For some reason, the phone number he was calling from wasn't showing up on my caller ID so I couldn't call him back. I wanted to talk to him and see how he was doing, hear his voice, and beg him to come home to me.

To us.

He sounded a little happier than the last time I heard his voice and that made me smile. It also thrilled me that he was calling. His letter had said he needed a clean break, yet here he was—calling me again.

It gave me hope. Maybe he had listened to what I said to him before he had left for New Zealand. Maybe he was having second thoughts. God, I needed him back here. I scrolled through my phone contacts, finding the number of one of the only two people in New Zealand that I could call.

Nervously, I tapped the call button and several seconds later, the phone began ringing. I hadn't considered what I was going to say to her if she answered.

The thought barely processed in my mind, when a heavily accented woman's voice answered, *"Kia ora."*

Unsure of what the words meant exactly, I stuttered a simple "H-hello?"

I waited for a second, and the woman said, "Hello? Who's calling, please?"

I took a breath. "Hello, is this Iria?" I asked, not sure if I pronounced her name correctly or not.

"Yes, it is. May I help you?" she asked politely.

"Hello, my name is Zoey James. You don't know me, but I'm trying to reach Andy Tate, and this is the only phone number I have."

She laughed. "Ah, tattoo girl. Yes, of course. I know who you are."

Tattoo girl? What did that mean?

"Are you still there Zoey?"

"Yes. Sorry, I'm still here," I said as I snapped back from outer space. I was in the bad habit lately of spacing out. "I was trying to figure out why you called me tattoo girl." I laughed nervously.

"Ah, I guess A.J. didn't tell you about it yet then, eh."

"No, he didn't," I replied, still confused. *Get to the point, Zoey.* "That's actually why I'm calling you. I keep missing his calls, and his phone number is not showing up on my caller ID so I can't call him back. I know he's moved back into his house with you and your husband, and I found your number on his old phone. I hope it's okay that I called you."

I suddenly felt stalker-like.

"Of course, Zoey. It's nice to speak to you. A.J. has told us so much about you I feel like I already know you."

Really? My heart did a little flutter in my chest. "That's good to hear. Does he happen to be around so I might talk to him for a few minutes?"

"No. I'm sorry. He went to play rugby with Tamati and his team. You've just missed him."

I chuckled. "Looks like we're playing phone tag, then."

She laughed.

"Iria," I said timidly. "Is he doing alright?" I suddenly felt like I was putting her in the middle of something in which she might not want to be involved. She didn't know me. "Sorry, you don't need to answer that."

"It's fine, Zoey. I don't mind. He's doing okay. He has good days and bad days. The day he received the photo book from you was the worst."

My heart sank. It wasn't my intention to hurt him when I made the album, especially on his birthday.

"The next day, he went to his favorite tattoo shop and had your name tattooed on his side."

What the? "He did?" *My name inked on his body . . . Forever . . .*

"Yeah, he did. He loves you very much."

I sighed with relief. "Thank you, Iria. I needed to hear that. Will you tell him I called, please? I'll be out of town for a couple of days but I'd love it if he would call me back."

"Of course, Zoey. Please call me anytime to talk, if you want to. I think we'll be good friends."

I heard the smile in her voice then I thanked her, and we ended the call.

What a whirlwind of emotions already today. I flopped down flat on my back in the middle of my bed, taking advantage of it, because when my belly grew bigger, I wouldn't be able to do it.

James hopped up on the bed with me, curled up in a ball right next to me, and fell asleep. I dozed off too.

I woke from my nap when my phone pinged with a text. I picked it up, surprised to see I had slept about an hour, and the text was from Iria.

The text contained a photo of Andy that he obviously didn't know she'd taken.

He was standing outside, shirtless, and was taking a drink from a bottle of water. It appeared he was taking a break from the rugby game Iria said he was playing.

He looked like he'd lost some weight, but the main thing I did notice, was the very large, very black tattoo running down the side of his torso, from just under his arm, to a few inches above his hipbone.

It simply said *Zoey.*

The style of the lettering seemed to match the Maori style of the rest of his tattoos. I couldn't believe he'd inked my name onto his body. I scrolled down to the bottom of the picture where Iria had sent a text message.

Thought you would want to see it for yourself.

I sent her a thank you text . . . and cried. Holding it together until I saw him again was going to be difficult, but the bigger picture was I had to take care of myself, our baby, and I needed to get answers about Emma. Until I had what we needed, there was no other choice for me but to let Andy do what he needed to cope.

Just before noon the next day, I hopped in my car to pick up Sasha so we could get on the road to San Francisco. The second I left my apartment, the butterflies started in my stomach. I was scared of what was coming, and scared of the information we would hopefully acquire from Michelle.

When I pulled up in front of Sasha's house, I honked the horn to let her know I was there. A few minutes later, she came outside pulling a giant rolling suitcase behind her. I laughed and popped open the trunk for her then stepped out of my car to help her with it.

"Sash? You do realize we're only going to be gone twenty-four hours right?" I giggled as I watched her attempt to lift the suitcase on her own.

She blew her newly blonde hair out of her face in frustration. "Are you just going to stand there or are you going to help me?"

I stepped off the curb, picked up one side of the suitcase, and helped her hoist it into the trunk.

"What the hell is in here, a body?" I asked. "I think I just strained my spleen from lifting that damn thing."

She glared at me over the top of her designer shades. "Very funny, Zoey, it takes a lot of work to be me, you know?"

We weren't far into our trip before we needed to stop for road trip snacks. Apparently, Baby Tate thought I needed to eat an entire box of Dibs Peanut Butter ice cream snacks.

Okay, maybe it was two boxes.

Three and a half hours, four stops to use the bathroom, two snack stops, and one small traffic jam later, we finally pulled into our hotel.

We decided to splurge and booked a suite with all the amenities, so we could have a girl's night in to help me stay calm. We had valets and bellhops galore to attend to us, and I for one, was relieved not to deal with Sasha's suitcase again. After checking into our spacious room, we changed into our pajamas and ordered room service. Sasha turned on a movie and sprawled out across the king sized bed to wait for our food.

"Sash?" I said, after a while.

"Yeah, Z?" she said as she looked at me.

"Thanks . . . for everything."

She winked at me. "Anytime."

Once again, the butterflies fluttered in my stomach, because in less than a day, my life was forever going to be changed, regardless of the outcome of our meeting with Michelle.

Chapter Five

Zoey

The next day, I finally rolled out of bed after a night of tossing and turning. After taking a long bath to relax, I forced myself to do a manicure and pedicure so I would be presentable when meeting Andy's ex-wife. I'd decided to attend the appointment with Michelle since mine and Andy's child was the motive for the meeting. I needed to hear for myself if Andy's genes or DNA was the cause of Emma's death. I also needed to learn the reasons for doing what she did directly from her mouth, not secondhand from Sasha.

While I was painting my toes, Sasha giggled, and I could sense she was trying to keep the atmosphere relaxed for me.

"You won't be able to do that too much longer on your own, Z."

I screwed the top onto my nail polish and dropped it back in my makeup bag. I laughed as I fanned my wet toes. She was right. I never thought about any of those things after my miscarriage. Little tasks like painting my toes, then eventually, not being able to *see* my feet.

"Guess I'll need to treat myself to the salon when the time comes."

I stood and suddenly had a very odd feeling low in my belly. Like a hundred little butterflies flitting around inside me. I rested my palms on my stomach and looked down to see if I could see it move. I let out a laugh for being a dumbass. Of course, I wouldn't be able to see it move yet. It was much too soon for that, but I definitely *felt* something.

"Zoey, is everything okay?" A very worried Sasha jogged across the room to me.

"Yeah, I'm fine," I whispered. Tears of both joy and sadness welled up in my eyes. "I think I just felt the baby move, Sash."

She smiled sympathetically and hugged me, not quite sure what to say to keep me from crying. It still didn't make my heart hurt any less. Andy was missing it, and all I wanted to do was break down and cry.

I needed to get this day over with, because as soon as possible, I was getting my pregnant ass—should I say, pregnant belly—on a plane to New Zealand to go get Andy and bring him home. I refused to deliver the news to him, regardless of whether it was good, or bad, over the phone. We'd need one another's support either way.

I changed into a fitted, knee length, red dress, and my favorite heels. I didn't want to meet Andy's ex-wife looking like a frumpy, pregnant chick who didn't care about her appearance. I applied my makeup while Sasha braided my hair in to a loose French braid, leaving several wavy tendrils hanging loose. Swinging the long braid to rest over my shoulder, Sasha gave me a once over.

She pulled a tiny box from her suitcase and handed it to me. "Here, you need to wear these too."

Carefully, I opened the box, which held a pair of diamond earrings that matched my engagement ring.

"Wow, Sash. Where did you get these?"

A love struck grin spread across her face. "Ben."

Apparently my tiny intrusion in her love life months ago worked. I knew they'd been dating since then, but I didn't realize they had become so serious.

"Aww, Sasha, that's awesome. But are you sure you don't mind me borrowing them?"

She shook her head and pushed me in front of the mirror. "Put them in now. But I swear, if you lose them, I will gut you and leave your body to rot on the side of the road."

God she was so gross sometimes. I laughed at her morbid sense of humor as I put in the earrings and handed the box back to her. I grabbed a sweater to go over my dress as the bellhop knocked on the door to collect our bags.

"It's go time," I said. We gathered our purses and headed to the elevator.

Forty-five minutes later, we pulled into the parking garage of the skyscraper where Michelle's real estate firm was located. Sasha found a parking space and shut off the car.

"Thank you for not crashing my baby," I said as I patted the dashboard of my Audi. I had forced Sasha to drive because my legs were trembling too badly from nerves.

She tossed my keys at me, and I dropped them into my purse.

We entered the building and headed straight for the elevator. The doors slid open and several people exited as we waited for our chance to enter. People in business suits carrying an array of briefcases and laptop bags filed in ahead of us. When it was finally our turn, Sasha needed to give me a little shove to get me to move.

I stepped inside and turned to face the door. *Breathe Zoey . . . Just breathe.*

Sasha filed into the crowded elevator next to me.

When the doors closed, and the car began to rise, my stomach dropped, and I swayed a bit from the movement. I immediately brought my hand up to my stomach and rubbed small circles over it. For some reason, it soothed me. I felt like Andy was with me, giving me the strength to continue.

The elevator stopped on a few floors, letting people off and on. It finally came to a stop on our floor, and again, my feet refused to move forward.

Sasha gave me another shove through the doors. "Move your ass, Z," she growled. She pulled me along behind her until we came to a vast lobby where a receptionist sat behind a large desk. She dropped my hand and walked to the desk where she gave the receptionist her name.

"Ladies, please take a seat," the receptionist said politely. "Michelle will be with you shortly."

We sat in an incredibly stylish waiting area with contemporary white leather chairs. The area was very clean and uncluttered with brightly colored artwork on the walls. There was also one entire wall with floor to ceiling windows, where you could see down to the Golden Gate Bridge.

We waited in silence until a petite Asian woman came to the lobby and called Sasha's name.

"Good afternoon. My name is Pam. Michelle can see you now. Please follow me," she said as we stood.

She led us down a wide hallway, with generous sized offices on either side.

Like the lobby area, the offices had front and back glass walls. I could easily see myself being nauseated if I stepped too close to the outside glass walls and looked down.

Pam stopped in front of one of the doors of the glass-encased offices and motioned for us to go in.

We went inside and there she was, sitting behind a large, glass-topped desk. One look at her confirmed my suspicions that she was the mysterious woman who showed up at the shop looking for Andy.

Noah had forgotten one major detail though. Michelle was gorgeous.

She rose from her chair and introduced herself to Sasha. She was wearing a gray, pencil skirt with a pale pink, low cut silk shirt.

Her short, dark hair was perfectly styled, and her makeup flawlessly accented her fair skin and brown eyes. She was exactly the opposite of me.

I realized Michelle had her hand extended and was introducing herself to me.

"Hello, Zoey," she said courteously after I told her my name.

I shook her hand and released it quickly, mumbling a hello. When I made eye contact with her, I noticed something in her eyes change.

We sat across from her, and she spoke with Sasha, asking her what type of property she was interested in purchasing. I was simply a friend that Sasha had brought along for "her" meeting with Michelle. When the time was right, one of us would start our inquisition.

As they talked, I casually glanced around her office to see if I could find anything out about her just by looking. I didn't see anything personal.

No photos, no nothing.

I turned my attention back to Sasha and Michelle who were discussing whether Sasha was going to be living by herself, or with someone.

My cell phone rang in my purse, startling me. I had meant to turn off the ringer, but my anxiety caused me to forget.

"Oh, I'm so sorry!" I pulled out my phone to silence it.

When I glanced at the screen, I saw it was a call I was waiting for. One call I would not, and could not afford to miss. Sasha and Michelle watched me as I fumbled with my phone. Thank God I had forgotten to shut off the ringer.

"It's my doctor, I need to take this." I offered my apologies again to both women for the interruption. I knew Sasha would wait for my return and then we would get down to business, and the true reason we were here.

As I pushed the glass door of Michelle's office open and stepped into the hallway, I answered my phone.

"Hello." I was so nervous it felt like the wind had been knocked out of me.

"Zoey, it's Dr. Stewart, how are you feeling?"

"I'm doing well, thank you," I replied as my pulse thrummed in my ears. I was facing the office where Michelle and Sasha sat, watching me curiously.

"Is everything okay, Dr. Stewart?"

The suspense was killing me about my test results. Since we didn't know what caused Emma's death, she had performed standard genetic testing, until we were sure of what to test for specifically. Once I had that information, they would perform a test for that particular condition.

Slowly, I paced back and forth, rubbing my hand over my small baby bump. I listened as the doctor told me all my tests had come back normal. Oh, thank you God.

I let out a long sigh, almost as if I had been holding my breath since I found out I was pregnant. Tears pricked my eyes from my sudden wave of relief. I glanced back into the office, immediately getting the impression that Michelle and Sasha were talking about me.

I stopped pacing and listened to the doctor as she continued to speak to me about my tests. I asked Dr. Stewart if it was okay for me to fly to New Zealand. She said it was, but she wanted to see me before I left. While we were on the phone, we confirmed my next appointment for the last week in September.

It would be my eighteen-week appointment, and I might get to find out if we were having a boy or a girl, but it would mean waiting another three weeks before I could tell Andy. I hated having to wait so long to tell him. However, Dr. Stewart promised me that if they had any appointment cancellations, they would get me in sooner.

I peeked back into the office at Sasha and Michelle again. They seemed to be having a slightly heated conversation about something. I ended the call and reached out to pull the office door open when Sasha abruptly stood and barged out of the office.

"What the heck happened?"

She stopped in front of me. "Zoey, she wants to talk to you."

What the hell.

"She knows who you are."

Oh shit. *Pull it together Zoey. You can do this.*

I returned to Michelle's office and stood behind the chairs we had been sitting in.

She spoke first.

"I thought you looked familiar when you came in, but I didn't realize who you were until you took your call."

She wasn't being rude, just to the point. I sat down on the chair and took a breath to speak.

"What do you want from me?" she asked before I could say anything.

"I need to know about Emma." I got straight to the point as she had with me.

She sucked in a breath and sat down. "Emma is none of your business."

I leaned toward her, resting my palms on her desk. "That's where you're wrong, Michelle." I took a deep breath. "I am very sorry for the loss of your child, but if there is something that I can do to prevent the loss of *mine* . . . please tell me what happened to her."

As angry as I was, I was not opposed to begging if it got me the information I needed.

Her eyes widened and traveled down to my stomach, then to my left hand.

Her eyes snapped back up to mine. "How far along are you?"

"Around fifteen weeks."

She slumped a little bit in her chair. "My family was against our relationship right from the beginning and they constantly put pressure on me to divorce him. I caved and left because I couldn't stand it any longer. I found out I was pregnant a month after I left him."

It made me sick to hear about her and Andy together, so I raised my hand to prevent her from going any further. "Look, I don't need to know about any of this. I really, truly believe your marriage to him is none of my business. I only need to know if our baby is going to be okay."

She nodded and took a deep breath. "Zoey, you need to understand how hard this is for me. *I lost my child.* I've made so many mistakes, but I do want to help you. I honestly didn't know why he came to see me before, but I just couldn't talk to him. I didn't know anything until I spoke to my brother. He admitted that he saw him and told him about Emma. I never told my family he didn't know about her."

She plucked a tissue from the box on her desk and dabbed her eyes.

"I knew I needed to talk to him once I found out what my brother had done, so I tracked him down and went to see him. He didn't answer the door of his apartment so I went to the shop below to find him. One of the men who worked there said he would locate him and asked me to wait in an office. I saw the photo of you together on the desk. He looked so happy with you and I didn't want to hurt him . . . so I left."

God, if only she'd stayed. I could have talked to her then, instead of sitting here, while Andy was suffering in New Zealand. Why couldn't she have stayed? Andy would know about Emma and our baby if she had and he might be home by now, or I would be there with him.

She dabbed her eyes again and shifted uncomfortably in her seat.

I was getting a little bit impatient with her. I didn't need to hear anything other than our baby was going to be born healthy, but I listened anyway. If any of what she was saying was going to help me, I would willingly listen.

"As soon as I found out I was pregnant, I knew I wanted to be with him and our baby, so I confided in my mother. She isn't the most forthcoming person or the nicest, for that matter. What she failed to tell my brother and I as we grew up, was that she gave birth to three other children, but they all died shortly after they were born."

I waited silently for her to continue her story. I felt sympathy for her, because she had lost a child and no mother should ever have to go through that. But, what she did to Andy was unforgivable. Not that it was up to *me* to forgive her.

"Sorry, I know I'm rambling," she admitted. "Emma died because of a hereditary gene in my family. It had nothing to do with Andy. As soon as my mother told me about her other children, I underwent several tests . . . they came back positive. That was when I decided he was better off not knowing about her. I knew Emma wouldn't survive and I had to live with that knowledge for seven months."

Oh God, that poor woman. Having lost a child in my first trimester when I was married to Rob was one of the most traumatic experiences of my life. I could not imagine going through seven months of a pregnancy, every day feeling the child you loved moving around inside you, and knowing what the outcome would be. At that moment, my heart truly ached for Michelle.

Tears fell from her eyes and slipped down her cheeks as she tried to keep her composure. She quickly wiped her tears away with her fingers, pushed her chair back, and stood.

"I think you should go now."

Finally, we had answers. I let out a sigh of relief and felt like driving to the airport that minute.

"Thank you, Michelle. I know you didn't have to tell me anything, but I appreciate that you did. I just wish you'd told Andy about her. It would have saved a lot of heartache for him by finding out the way he did."

Michelle nodded once and looked down, appearing remorseful and a big weight seemed to be lifted off her shoulders.

She opened the top drawer of her desk, pulled out a manila envelope, and held it out to me. "Will you give this to him, please?"

I took it. "Yes, of course. Thank you for talking to me." I grabbed my purse and hurried to the door.

She called my name and I turned to face her.

"You're very brave, Zoey." She eyed me inquisitively. "I wish I could've been as brave as you. Congratulations on your baby."

"Thank you, for everything." I turned and pushed through the door and never looked back. I found Sasha waiting in the lobby for me in one of the white leather chairs. As soon as she saw me, she scrambled to her feet.

"Zoey, oh my God! What happened?"

I opened my purse, shoved the envelope inside it, and grabbed her hand.

"Let's go Sash . . . I need to get out of here, now."

Adrenaline raced through my body as we rushed toward the elevator. Even in a building made of windows, I felt as if I was suffocating in that place. I was relieved with the news Michelle gave me, but I was at a breaking point and needed fresh, cold air.

We reached the elevator just as the doors were inches away from closing. Sasha sacrificed herself by putting her hand in between the doors, forcing them to reopen. Which in turn, pissed off the people inside it.

Oh well, get over it assholes. We're on a mission here.

We crammed ourselves into the very full elevator and high-fived each other. Sasha looked over at me questioningly as she entwined her fingers with mine.

I just smiled and nodded, indicating to her that I'd acquired what we came for. I loved my best friend so much at that moment for helping me.

We finally made our way back down to the parking garage and sat in my car where I spilled the entire conversation between Michelle and me. I reclined my seat back as far as it would go so I could relax and calm my nerves. I laid back, relieved, and completely overwhelmed at all the news I'd received.

Baby Tate would be perfectly healthy. I knew it in my heart.

"Let's get the hell out of this town, Sash. I have a trip to plan," I said, a few seconds before my stomach growled embarrassingly loud.

"We need food too." She laughed at me and took me out for an early celebratory dinner.

Chapter Six

Zoey

Reclining back on the exam table for my eighteen-week ultrasound, my mom settled in the chair next to me.

"Let's see if we can get this little guy, or girl, to cooperate today," Dr. Stewart said as she squirted gel on my ever-growing belly.

It was official; I looked like I had swallowed half a basketball. I hadn't gained much weight since my previous appointment, but I was eating well and taking care of myself. Since I had found out all the information I needed from Michelle, my stress level was next to nothing. I still took time to myself each day so I wouldn't have any setbacks and slip into my old ways, but it was getting better every day.

When I had found out I was pregnant, I wanted to jump on a plane right then and fly to New Zealand, but with my stubbornness of handling everything on my own, I couldn't leave right away. I had to train both of my parents on how to take care of the day to day business at the store because I'd been doing it all on my own. Between them working behind the scenes and my employee, Tara, taking care of keeping the store stocked and orders up to date, I now felt comfortable leaving everything behind in their capable hands.

Even though I had to wait nearly a month to get my affairs in order, I missed Andy like crazy, but we had talked a few times on the phone. I was also becoming good friends with Iria, just as she said we would. She was a huge help in planning my trip to New Zealand.

She hadn't told Andy I was coming, but Iria told Tamati so he could keep Andy busy on the day of my arrival. I hated all the secrecy, but what choice did I have? There was no way for me to know what Andy would do if he knew I was coming to New Zealand. Would he leave? Would he be angry that I came, or happy to see me? I just couldn't risk him knowing.

Iria and Tamati backed me up one-hundred percent that telling him beforehand would not be a good idea in his state of mind. Andy was miserable and grieving, but they knew I had the information he needed about Emma. They were keeping an eye on him and trying to keep him busy.

I focused back to the task at hand. Looking at the screen, I found Baby Tate was bouncing around inside me. It was a very strange sensation to see it on the screen and feel it inside me at the same time.

Dr. Stewart moved the wand around on my belly for a minute or so and then stopped. "Looks like we have a good view here, Zoey, would you like to know what you're having?"

Glancing over at my mom for reassurance, I nodded to the doctor. "Yes, please, more than anything." I wanted Andy there with me, but I honestly couldn't wait to find out. I'd been anxious for days about my appointment, because it signified my last hurdle before I left my family and friends behind and went into the unknown. I swore right then, that everything else in regards to our baby, Andy would be right there beside me. That is, if he wanted to be.

Dr. Stewart smiled up at me. "It's a girl."

Of course, my mom and I both started crying happy tears. We'd be adding another baby girl to the family. Jason and Heather's little girl, Mya, had been born last June, the day after Jess and Noah's wedding. Her Auntie Zoey and her grandma spoiled her rotten.

After a few minutes, I asked Dr. Stewart if it was still okay for me to fly to New Zealand.

"Yes, I think you'll be just fine," she said. "When do you plan on coming back?"

I honestly didn't know when I would be returning. For all I knew, our baby girl would be born in New Zealand. I would come back when Andy was ready to, and not a minute sooner. "I'm not really sure yet."

"You've had a very healthy pregnancy so far, but try not to fly back in your last month. I'll ask the girls in the office to copy your medical records, and you can take them with you."

For the entire week prior to my appointment, I had been packing and tying up loose ends before my trip. I also did some shopping for bigger clothing since I didn't know how long I was going to be away. I researched online and discovered since it was the beginning of spring in New Zealand, the weather would be significantly cooler than here. I packed my raincoat and some rain boots at Iria's suggestion because it would most definitely rain while I was there.

After a goodbye brunch with my family and friends, I would be leaving for New Zealand to see *him*. I was not looking forward to being on a plane for over twelve hours at once, but I was going to see Andy again. I would swim if I had to.

I knew exactly how he felt when I was in Cabo. I couldn't wait to see him, and finally tell him the news of our baby girl. I hoped everything would go according to plan and he would come home with me.

After my luggage was packed, I changed into my leisurely traveling outfit of a stretchy, but cute cotton dress.

While I was getting ready, I found myself chanting "seventeen hours" over and over in my head.

Once I stepped onto the first plane, it would be seventeen hours from here, to where he was. I took the shortest, quickest flight I could get which put my arrival in New Zealand at six-thirty in the morning. I would have preferred to arrive in Auckland in the evening, but that would have increased the travel time to anywhere between twenty-six, to over forty hours and there was no way my constantly changing body could handle that many hours of travel.

As previously ordered, I walked next door and knocked on Will and Justin's door so they could take my luggage to my car for me. James followed me over because he knew I was leaving him anytime I brought out a suitcase. He proceeded to curl up underneath their coffee table and fall asleep.

As they loaded the luggage into my car, I packed my iPod, my new Kindle that was loaded with e-books, and some snacks in the enormous purse that Sasha convinced me I needed for my trip. I chuckled as I remembered the last time I'd carried a ginormous purse. I'd accidently dumped its entire contents in Andy's truck only to have everything fall all over his feet when he'd opened the door.

The boys and I drove to my parents' house in my car. As soon as we walked through the door, my nephew Jake ran over to feel my belly.

"*Hola,* baby cousin!" he yelled at my stomach.

I felt a twitch inside. "Jakey, I think she heard you." The movements inside me were getting stronger and stronger every day. A twinge of guilt filled my heart because Andy should have been experiencing it right along with me.

We greeted everyone as Jake and I worked our way through the house. As soon as I saw Heather, I begged her to let me hold Mya. She was almost four months old and absolutely gorgeous.

I sat down on the edge of the couch with her and rocked her gently while she looked around the room. "Heather, can you take a picture of me with her and the boys?"

"Of course," she replied with a smile.

Jake and Alex both crowded in on either side of me while Heather took the picture with my cell phone.

Since I had made Andy the photo album for his birthday, I'd officially decided I was going to be taking pictures of everything and filling albums with them. On each page, I would fill out a postcard with a written memory, or one of my favorite song lyrics.

The day I found out I was pregnant, I started a new album. I took a photo of myself every week of my pregnancy, so we could see the progression of my expanding waistline.

I didn't want Andy to miss anything. Even that.

After Heather took baby Mya into a bedroom to feed her and put her down for a nap, I sat on the couch and put my feet up. I was tired from the last three days of packing and errands and my doctor's appointment.

I pulled out my cell phone and looked over the picture Heather snapped. Since it didn't show my belly, I sent it to Andy, and told him how much the family missed him. Then I laid back to relax. Of course, I dozed off for a few minutes. Well, maybe longer than a few minutes. I woke to my dad shaking my shoulder lightly.

"Baby girl, food's ready," he said quietly.

I sat up and slipped my shoes back on as my phone pinged with a text from Andy.

> I can't believe how much Mya has grown. And you, Zoey, I've never seen you looking more beautiful. You're a wonderful aunt. Someday you'll be a wonderful mum . . .

The thought of him saying that broke my heart. God, if he only knew. I needed to tell him, *soon.* I sent him a text back.

> You are going to be the most loving, wonderful father a little girl could ever ask for.

He wouldn't know the real significance of my words, but it was my way of telling him, without revealing the truth to him until I could in person.

I knew he wouldn't message me back afterward, and he didn't. He was still hurting. I hoped by tomorrow night, everything would be out in the open. I put my phone away and sat down to eat with my family and friends. We talked about my trip and life in general while we ate.

When it was time to leave for the airport, I checked my giant purse for my passport, the envelope from Michelle, my medical records, the photo album I was making, and DVD's of my sonograms. Those five items were critical to my plan so I could not lose them. If I lost my luggage, I wouldn't care because I would still have my purse containing everything that would bring Andy home.

I had no idea what was in the envelope from Michelle. I knew that whatever it was, it would make sense to Andy, and it would hopefully give him some sort of closure to that part of his life.

"Z, you alright back there?" Justin asked from the front seat as Will drove us to the airport.

"Yeah, I'm good. I just can't believe this day is finally here."

He smiled at me with empathy in his eyes. "I know this last month has been really hard for you, but it's made you a true warrior."

He laughed as I stared at him like he was crazy.

"A warrior, huh?" A smile formed at the corners of my mouth.

"Make that a warrior *queen*," he joked.

From the driver's seat, Will laughed. "Honey, there are three queens in this car tonight. Wait, why the fuck am I driving?" he joked. "Shouldn't someone be driving us to the airport? Queens don't drive. They have minions for that."

Justin and I went in to hysterics at that point. I finally caught my breath and wiped my happy tears away.

"Can I be the only queen for a night? You guys can be my minions for a while. Just this once, I promise."

They both agreed as we pulled into the parking area at the airport. The car hadn't even come to a complete stop before Justin jumped out and opened my door for me.

"My queen," he said in a heavy British accent as he bowed and held his hand out to help me from the car.

"Thank you, kind sir," I responded in a very bad imitation of his perfect British accent.

Once I was all checked in, I had to say goodbye to them.

"Thank you guys for everything, I don't know how I could have done any of this without you. I can never repay you," I said as I hugged them.

"Good luck, Z. I love you," Justin said with big tears in his eyes.

After hugging them tight one last time, I told them how much I loved them, and walked away.

"Come on baby girl," I said as I rested my palm against my belly. "Let's go get your daddy and bring him home."

Once I arrived in the waiting area to board the plane, it hit me that I was on my own until I reached New Zealand, and I had never been more scared in my life.

My friends and family were so supportive of me, but it was time for me to go to Andy, and support him. He was devastated by his loss, but I had all the answers he needed. I hoped it would be enough, and he would come home with me. I was willing to give up everything to be with him and our daughter. I would give up my store, my apartment, and my life in Sacramento if I had to. Before Andy, I never would've considered it, but he and our little girl meant more to me than any possession.

Wanting to be alone with my thoughts, I found a seat away from everyone. I pulled my iPod out of my purse, set it to shuffle and people watched while I waited for the call to board the plane.

I was too nervous to do anything else.

As I waited for the plane to take me to *him,* the perfect song came on, and it helped calm my nerves. "Set Fire to the Third Bar" had the exact lyrics I needed to get me in the right mindset for my trip. The lyrics talked about looking at a map and being only inches away from the one you loved, but being so far away physically. I was just inches away from him on a map, but over six thousand miles separated us.

I played it a few times in a row, and by the time I moved on to the next song, I was feeling more confident with my decisions. People began stirring around me, so I took my earbuds out and put my iPod away.

It was time to board the plane.

Chapter Seven

Zoey

Once I settled in my seat and had my purse safely stowed under the seat in front of me, I sent Iria a text letting her know I was on the plane. The plane was crowded, but the seat in the middle of my row wasn't filled. There was an older man in the aisle seat, and I was by the window, so both of us had plenty of room to stretch out.

One good thing about being pregnant, I was tired a lot of the time and no longer had issues sleeping. Throughout the entire flight, I spent my time reading or napping. And of course, walking around to stretch my legs on my several trips to the bathroom. I felt a little bad for the poor guy next to me because he had to get up each time I did.

After finishing my book, I dozed off again, and before I knew it, we were preparing to land in Auckland. My heart was thumping so hard by the time we arrived at our gate, I thought it was going to thump right out of my chest.

It was still dark outside, but the sun was lighting up the horizon in the distance. I held my purse tightly, said goodbye to my neighbor, and exited the plane.

Getting through customs was a nightmare. It took forever. I chuckled to myself and wished my minions had come to help me with my bags as I moved at a snail's pace while weaving my way through the roped off lines. I'd need to punish them later because they failed in their duties as my minions. Just as I finished up with the customs representative, my phone pinged with a text from Iria saying she was waiting for me.

Eventually, I found her holding a big sign that said,

> *Zoey!*
> *Welcome to*
> *En Zed!*

While Iria and I had been becoming friends, I learned many great things from her about New Zealand, including slang words and general phrases. I laughed when I thought how if anyone here were to call me Z, like everyone did at home, they would probably say "Zed" instead since that was how New Zealanders pronounced the letter Z.

I waved at Iria excitedly. She was a stunning Maori woman with long dark hair and beautiful dark eyes and skin. She took one look at me and her mouth dropped open as her eyes fell to my small bump.

"Zoey, I think you forgot to tell me something," she said as she stared at my belly.

I stopped in front of her. "I know . . . and I am so sorry for not telling you, but *this* is the reason I'm here. You were already keeping so many secrets for me about this trip I couldn't burden you with this one too."

She nodded in understanding, and then proceeded to hug me. "*Kia ora,* Zoey. I'm glad you're finally here."

"Thank you, I'm glad I'm finally here," I said with a nervous laugh. "I am ready for everything to be out in the open."

We loaded my bags into her car and Iria told me that by the time we arrived at the house, Andy and Tamati would be gone for the day. They were going to play rugby and then go fishing. They would get home later in the evening, so I would have the whole day to settle in and prepare for what was to come.

Iria drove for an hour after leaving the airport. I didn't realize how big the city of Auckland actually was. She was driving through a nice neighborhood when she glanced over at me.

"Zoey, do you want to see him right now?"

I shook my head, but my mouth instinctively said, "Yes."

We laughed and several minutes later, a large park appeared. She wedged her little car in between two SUV's.

"Don't worry, he won't see us from here," she promised.

We stepped out of the car and shielded ourselves from the view of the men on the rugby field.

"I feel like a stalker," I joked.

Iria laughed and nodded in agreement.

I would just have to feel like a stalker for a while because I needed to see that he was here, in the flesh. My heart clenched in my chest at the sight of him because I had missed him so much.

Iria explained the game to me as we watched.

"He's really good, isn't he?" I asked her, unable to peel my eyes away from my man on the field.

"Yeah, he is. Tamati said he could've gone pro eventually, but he moved to the States."

I had no idea. I knew they were driving home from his rugby game when the car accident happened. Not only had his family been taken from him, but his chance of playing pro rugby had as well.

My heart ached for him even more.

The ball was tossed to Andy, and he ran down the field, dodging guys on the opposite team.

Unexpectedly, he slowed just enough and turned his head to look in our direction. Not a split second later, he was hit by two guys and knocked hard to the ground.

Those two guys were followed by about four more, and they all ended up in a big pile right on top of Andy.

I started to panic, thinking he might be hurt, but Iria said, "Don't worry. That's normal for this game."

As soon as the words left her mouth, the ball reappeared from beneath the mountain of men, and the game continued as if nothing had happened.

I backed up between the cars again while Andy picked himself up, and took off running. He stopped suddenly, glanced back in our direction then followed his teammates down the field again.

"That was close," I said as we hopped back in the car and sped off down the road. "Rugby is a crazy game. I can't believe they just tackle each other like that, with no helmets or anything on."

She shrugged her shoulders and laughed. "Kiwi men are the toughest," she said with a proud smile.

"I'll second that. Makes me think our American football players are a bunch of wimps in all their protective gear."

She nodded in agreement. "Ask A.J. what it feels like to take a boot straight to the face. He has the scar to prove it."

"A boot to the face?"

"Yeah, the scar on his nose is from the bottom of a rugby boot. Tamati said he got it back in school. He was kicked in the face, went off the field to get it fixed up, spent some time in the sin bin for punching the guy that kicked him, then went right back to playing."

Ouch . . . I had assumed that scar came from the accident like the others, not from playing rugby.

On the drive, I noticed how green everything was, almost tropical, but not really . . . *tropical*. It was different from any other place I'd been, but very similar to the Northern California coast with its mix of ferns, trees, and flowering plants. We were getting in to an area where the houses became bigger and more upscale as we drove. I noticed several signs with names I wasn't sure how to pronounce, like Takapuna and Minehaha. Everything around me was becoming a blur.

Iria pulled the car in through a gated driveway and parked in front of two large garage doors. The house was huge, the top floor mostly windows and large glass doors. There was a covered patio area on the second floor with a mid-sized table and chairs set up for dining outside.

This is Andy's place? Holy crap.

Apparently, we entered the property from the rear, because when we reached the living room, I noticed the entire front of the house was glass and it overlooked the ocean.

"Wow," I said as I approached the windows. I was completely awestruck.

The house didn't merely overlook the ocean. It was *on* the freaking beach!

"This place is amazing," I said to Iria.

There was a light, cream-colored sectional couch with a chaise lounge on one end and two matching chairs set up around a large coffee table. In the center of the table was a large basket of seashells and starfish. Looking around, I saw the entire house had a beach theme to it.

Andy previously told me he lived a charmed life growing up, but I didn't know how charmed.

"So this was his parents' house?"

Iria came up to admire the breathtaking view with me. "Yeah, this is where he grew up. We moved in a few years ago, but he's been renting it out ever since he moved to the States. We've updated some of the furniture, but for the most part, it's exactly the way it was when he lived here. Would you like a tour?"

Heck yes. "I'd love one, actually."

She showed me the state of the art kitchen and all the rooms downstairs first then took me upstairs to the bedrooms. We entered a mid-sized bedroom plastered with rugby paraphernalia.

"This room belonged to A.J. when he was young. The family who rented it before us had a little boy who loved the room so much they didn't take anything off the walls."

The entire room was dedicated to the All Blacks, New Zealand's very famous, professional rugby team.

"He sure loves his rugby doesn't he?" I laughed.

Iria laughed with me. "There is not a person in this country who isn't obsessed with the Blacks, Zoey."

She finished our tour in Andy's current bedroom, which had a large bed and a spacious bathroom with a spa tub and tile shower. I would definitely be using that tub later.

My stomach picked that moment to growl loudly. So loud, we both burst out laughing.

"Zoey, let me make you something to eat while you get settled in. I'm sure you're tired too. Please, make yourself at home."

She was right about that. I was tired, and hungry. A brief thought passed through my mind about how I was always hungry now, and never forgot to eat. I would have to tease Andy a little bit because I was definitely carrying *his* child. That man could flat-out eat.

Once I'd unpacked a few things I would need for the day, I met Iria back in the kitchen where she had prepared a mouthwatering salad with lamb for us. I hadn't had real food since my brunch the day before with my family. We talked while we ate, and when we were finished, I helped with the dishes, and then excused myself to go take a bath and change. While I was waiting for the water to fill the tub, I called my parents and let them know I'd arrived safely.

I soaked in the bathtub until my fingers were wrinkly, then dressed in a pair of my new jeans and a cute wrap-around turquoise top that hugged my growing belly in all the right places. I wasn't tired anymore, so I dried my hair and put on a bit of makeup before I went to find Iria. I plopped down on the couch next to her.

For several days, I'd been thinking of ways to tell Andy about our baby that would hopefully take away the heaviness of our conversation about Emma. My priority was to give him all the information I had regarding her first. Understandably, he would be devastated, but I didn't want the news of our little one to be minimized.

Just blurting out that I was pregnant didn't feel right, so I wanted to do something unique to tell him. Since his wish was to have a child by his thirtieth birthday, I considered buying him an early gift. After thinking about how his childhood bedroom was still decorated, I stood and stretched because I'd finally figured out what to buy him.

"Iria, is there anywhere I can get an All Blacks baby outfit?"

She nodded with a knowing smile. "Champions of the World. They'll have everything you need there."

While we shopped, I picked out a tiny onesie, some PJ's with the All Blacks logo on them, and some matching baby booties. I couldn't resist the adorable stuffed teddy bear that wore its own All Blacks clothing and a team hoody for myself.

Suddenly, I was extremely nervous and feeling a little giddy being in New Zealand. "I don't suppose this comes in pink?" I whispered to Iria as I held up the onesie to show her.

She shook her head and laughed heartily. "No, looks like your little girl will be wearing *all black*."

Nice pun.

"You know what's funny? I haven't bought anything for our baby yet. I wanted Andy to be there for every little thing, and the first thing I buy her is a rugby outfit."

She looked over at me with what appeared to be compassion in her eyes. "It sounds like you haven't had much time to do anything for yourself in the last month Zoey, with as busy as you've been."

That was a fact.

"It's getting late," she said as she glanced down at her watch. "We should get going."

Back at the house, we had a quiet dinner out on the deck overlooking the ocean before I decided to call it a night. The anticipation of seeing Andy weighed heavily on me, and getting some sleep before he came home would hopefully give me the strength to do what I needed to do. I had no idea how he would react when he found out I was there, but I knew it would be a long night.

After I changed into a loose nightgown, I gathered up the items I needed for when Andy arrived and slipped into his bed, breathing in the scent from his pillow. I had missed him so much. I laid on the bed, going over in my head for the hundredth time, how I was going to tell him all I had to say.

Of course, I wanted to tell him about our baby first, but I knew that in order to keep him from completely losing it, I had to put Emma first. He needed to know the cause of her death had nothing to do with him.

Then it would be time to tell him about our baby girl.

Andy

"This was a good idea, mate. I needed this today," I said to Tamati as we hoisted a large chilly bin full of ice and the fish we'd caught into the back of his Ute. We'd played a rugby game that morning and spent the rest of the day fishing.

"I've always got good ideas, bro." He chuckled and closed the tailgate. Once the chilly bin had been strapped down, we headed back to the house. "Iria is going to love all this fresh fish, and I can't wait for the first batch of fish and chips she cooks," he said with a proud grin.

He was right—she did make the best fish and chips. And meat pies, roast lamb, and venison stew. My stomach growled at the thought of all the traditional New Zealand food I had missed while living in the States.

It had been over a month since I'd arrived in Auckland. I was depressed, to say the least. The only good thing about being in Auckland was that I'd seen several doctors who'd performed every test imaginable to find out if there was anything physically wrong with me. I'd had blood tests, piss tests, scans, semen tests, and the obvious DNA testing since that was where my main concern was.

I spared no expense for the cost of the tests, and the doctors found nothing. Not a damn thing. Just a healthy twenty-nine year old man who was now trying to figure out a way to beg the love of his life in California for forgiveness. I'd only had the last of the test results given to me two days prior, and Tamati had taken me out to celebrate. I had plans to book a flight back to Sacramento the next day.

Zoey and I had been in contact a few times after she'd sent me the photo book for my birthday. She definitely made her point by making it and sending it to me. It was the reason I decided to see all the doctors and specialists. She was my life and I didn't want to live without her.

"Look, mate," Tamati said once we'd entered the kitchen through the garage, snapping my thoughts away from Zoey. "I've got something to tell you."

Just then, Iria came around the corner from the living room and she wore a concerned look on her face. Dread washed over me like a tidal wave and my immediate thought was that something had happened to Zoey.

"Sit down, A.J., please," Iria said as she took a seat at the table.

Tamati pulled two chairs out. When I didn't sit, he pulled me down onto the seat next to his. The hairs on the back of my neck stood on end and I felt my body begin to shake. "What's happened?" I asked, scared of her answer.

"It's Zoey." A hint of a smile touched the corners of Iria's mouth. "She's here."

She's here in En Zed? I drew in a deep breath, and caught the scent of her vanilla-lavender soap. "Where is she?" I asked anxiously and pushed my chair back to stand

and look around for her. Fuck, I almost felt faint. I didn't know if it was from shock or from not eating since lunchtime. Nobody answered me so I glanced back to Iria. "Where is she?" I repeated.

She squeezed my hand and smiled. Her eyes filled with tears. "She's asleep in your room."

The words were barely out of her mouth before I turned and headed for the stairs, running up them three at a time. Just outside my closed bedroom door, I paused to calm myself. What was I going to say to her? Why was she here? Would she forgive me? I placed the palm of my left hand on the door and silently said a prayer that she didn't hate me.

Quietly, I slipped inside the room and closed the door behind me.

"Zoey?" I whispered loud enough for her to hear me, but not startle her.

No response. I made my way over to the bathroom and flipped on the light inside. When I turned to face my bed, I was not prepared for what I saw. Her head was on my pillow, and her right arm wrapped around a pillow in front of her. Her golden blonde hair was loose, and part of it was fanned out on the pillow behind her while the rest hung over her shoulder and neck.

Carefully, I eased onto the bed next to her. I wanted to touch her and wake her up right then, but seeing her there in my bed caused a surge of emotion I hadn't expected. Embarrassed by my reaction, I had to cover my mouth so a sob didn't escape with the tear that trickled down my cheek. I couldn't force my eyes away from her. Her skin looked like porcelain with a slight rosiness to it, and her cheeks had filled in so her cheekbones weren't so visible. She looked perfect, healthy, and more beautiful than I'd ever seen her. She looked the same, yet so different.

She stirred when I pushed her hair back over her shoulder to get a better look at her. Her hair was so much softer than I'd remembered and her lips were perfectly pink. I dried my face with my sleeve and just stared at her. *Please open your eyes, Beautiful . . . let me see those baby blues.*

My wish was granted and Zoey slowly opened her eyes to meet mine.

Chapter Eight

Zoey

As soon as I woke up, I felt Andy's presence before my eyes even opened. I'd been dreaming about him running his fingers through my hair and across my skin, the way he had so many times before.

"Zoey, hey Beautiful. Wake up," he said in a calm, soothing voice mixed with emotion.

I breathed in, catching the unmistakable scent of Andy . . . and fish. I immediately started giggling. "You smell like fish, Sexy."

He laughed his deep, sexy laugh that was laced with nervousness. "I'm sorry . . . God, I can't believe you're here. What's going on? Are you okay? What are you doing here?" He rattled off questions so fast I couldn't answer him before he asked another. He finally stopped talking and brushed a lock of hair away from my face, staring down at me in wonder.

"I'm fine, perfect actually, now that I've seen you. I have a lot to tell you and I couldn't do it over the phone, so here I am." The smell of the fish on his clothes was actually making me a bit nauseous, so I chuckled. "But you really do stink like fish," I teased to keep the mood light.

He laughed and pulled the collar of his shirt up and gave it a sniff. "You're right. Let me go shower so I smell better. I'll be right back." Andy started to stand.

Fish stench or not, I needed to feel his lips on mine. Reaching out, I grabbed hold of his wrist. "Wait . . . come back here and kiss me. I've missed those lips of yours like crazy." I propped myself up on my elbow and he knelt down on the floor. I could barely make him out because the only light filtering into the room was coming from the bathroom. Plus, I knew he couldn't see my body very well with the large pillow in front of me.

He put his fishy hands behind his back and leaned forward to kiss me.

"These lips have missed you too. More than they could ever say," he whispered as he rested his forehead against mine.

Our lips hovered near each other without touching. I held his face in my hands and pulled him closer until our lips finally touched. We both paused, as if unsure of each other, lips touching for several seconds before I had to have more. I parted my lips and ran my tongue across his bottom lip.

That was all it took before our kiss was so involved, he began pulling the covers off to get into bed with me. Using all the mental strength I had, I broke the kiss and pulled the covers back up.

"Easy there, fish man," I said, out of breath. "You still need a shower."

Andy stood again. "I'll be right back."

He bent forward and kissed me again. "I'm happy you're here, Zoey. I have missed you so much. But you have lots of explaining to do."

He grinned as he backed up all the way to the bathroom, never taking his eyes off me.

While he showered, I set everything I'd brought with me on the nightstand. I needed to keep busy, but I ran out of things to do because I had been so well prepared. He had left the bathroom door open while he showered, so of course, I stood in the doorway and watched him through the misted shower doors in all his naked glory as he soaped up.

Thank God for glass showers, even though I could only see the outline of his gorgeous body. I felt safe standing there because I knew if I couldn't see him clearly, he couldn't see me very well either.

"I can feel you standing there, Beautiful," he said, after a few minutes.

We both let out a nervous laugh at the same time.

"Sorry," I said, even though I really wasn't. "You know I can't help myself. It's been too long since I've seen you."

He lathered his hair with shampoo. "You can always join me in here if you want to."

It was just like old times, for now. Over the time he had been away, I had forgiven him for leaving. My anger had turned to forgiveness and compassion for everything he'd gone through since finding out about Emma.

But, he had broken my heart when he left me, and I needed him to know that. Tonight wasn't the right time, so I'd save that talk for another day. The most important thing was for us to be back together, and for him to know about Emma and our baby.

As soon as he was done in the shower, everything was going to change. Hopefully for the better.

"I'll take you up on that shower invite tomorrow, okay?"

"Suit yourself," he said as he rinsed his hair.

I needed to get out of here before I climbed into the shower with him, like I had so many months ago. I needed to play this smart.

"Zoey, while you're in here watching me, can you bring me a towel please? I forgot to grab one."

Shit . . ."Yeah, just a minute."

As soon as I opened the door of the towel closet, he shut off the water. *Shit!*

My nightgown was loose, but if it pulled against me the tiniest little bit . . . I didn't know what to do, so I grabbed the entire stack of towels. I carried them in front of me over to where he was standing, naked, dripping all over the rug on the floor outside the shower.

He watched me curiously with his eyebrow raised. Dear God, he looked incredibly sexy when he did that.

"I only need one," he joked as he took a towel off the top of the stack.

I smiled at him, taking in the sight of his entire body. He was breathtakingly beautiful, and I had missed him more than I ever thought possible.

As I turned away, he snaked his arm out and pulled me close to kiss me, smashing the stack of towels between us. We kissed so desperately, I actually let go of them to wrap my arms around his wet body.

The droplets of water raining down on my face from his hair got my attention.

Shit, Zoey, snap out of it. I let go of him and took hold of the towels again so they wouldn't fall.

He pulled back. "What's going on with you?" he asked suspiciously, doing that sexy eyebrow-raising thing again.

Out of breath, I let out a small laugh. "Well, according to you, I have lots of explaining to do. I'll just wait for you in your bedroom."

I turned around to exit the bathroom still carrying the towels. I dropped them on the dresser and jumped back in bed before he could see me.

Settling myself on a couple of pillows against the headboard, I pulled the covers up around me. I went so far as to take an extra pillow and set it on my lap.

A few minutes later, he came out of the bathroom. Completely naked.

"Seriously, Andy, what is with you and nudity? Are you some sort of an exhibitionist or something?"

He laughed as he pulled the covers back to get in bed.

"Oh no you don't," I scolded and yanked the blankets out of his hand. I pointed to his dresser. "Clothes. Now! We have a lot to talk about before you're allowed in bed with no clothes."

"But it's my bed, I should get to wear what I want," he teased and propped his hands on his narrow hips.

Andy stood there, defiant, waiting for me to cave and let him into bed. He was going to lose this battle. *Just this once.*

"It might be your bed, but they're my rules for now and I need you to abide by them for me. Please?" God that man flustered me with his affinity for being nude. He knew what it did to me and always played it to his advantage, but damn it, we had very important things to discuss.

Tapping my fingers on the pillow that blocked my stomach, I scowled at him until he turned around and pulled some boxer briefs and shorts out of his dresser.

Once he put them on, he turned to face me. "Can I come to bed now?" He shot me a sinful grin as his blue eyes burned into mine. "Please?"

I pulled the covers back just enough for him to get in and patted the bed. "Yes, you can get in now that you're wearing the proper bedroom attire. By the way, I like your new tattoo." I stared at my name scrawled down his side.

"Thank you. She's a very special girl." He turned to the side to show me the tattoo.

"I still want my snowflakes, you know . . . and you never took me to get them." I gave him a hopeful look that I prayed would help the situation and let him know that I still wanted everything he'd promised me.

"Maybe I'll take you to get them while you're here," he said with a smile.

Uh no, definitely won't be getting any tattoos for a while.

Andy dropped onto the bed next to me and propped himself against the pillows. He looked at the stack containing Michelle's envelope and my medical records laying on the bed in front of me.

"What's all that?" He pointed to the items.

Before I responded, I thought for a second to make sure I chose my words carefully. "It's our past, present, and future," I said as I watched his expression go from happy to anxious in two seconds flat.

"Zoey . . ." He shifted his body toward me then took in a deep breath to speak.

"Wait," I said, so he wouldn't tell me we didn't *have* a future. "Please, you need to trust me. I have all the answers you've been waiting for, right here." I laid my hand on the papers. "So much has happened since you left. Can you let me do this the way I need to? It will all make sense."

I was trying to keep my emotions inside for the time being, but it was hard.

He nodded. "Yes, of course. I trust you with my life. You know that."

Then why did you leave me?

"No, I didn't know that," I whispered and looked down at the information that was going to change both our lives forever.

I chose the first thing he needed to know about. Emma.

I handed him the manila envelope from Michelle.

"What's in it?" He turned it over in his hands to open it.

"I'm actually not sure," I admitted honestly. "It's from Michelle. She asked me to give it to you."

To say that he was surprised was an understatement.

"You talked to Michelle?" he asked. "How did you get in to see her?"

"We made an appointment," I said bluntly.

He waited for an explanation, which I gave him. He was shocked, to say the least.

"Open the envelope," I urged.

He almost looked scared at what he might find inside and I was definitely scared to find out what was in it.

Once the seal was broken on the envelope, he carefully slid the contents out onto the bed. There were several folded papers and another smaller envelope. Andy stared nervously at the papers laying in front of him. He swallowed hard, and then brushed his knuckles over his jaw.

My heart was aching for him so badly I wanted to pull him into my arms and take all his sorrow away. I could tell simply by looking at him he hadn't been sleeping well. His eyes were slightly bloodshot with dark circles beneath them and he seemed exhausted.

"Andy, will you look at me please?" I waited for his blue eyes to meet mine, and when they did, I motioned toward the papers. "No matter what is in there, I want you to know I'm right here with you. Everything *will* work out. I swear it. You have to believe me."

He nodded and picked through the papers, looked them over, and then handed them to me when he was done with them.

The first paper he handed me was a copy of Emma's legal birth certificate from the State of California. His name wasn't listed in the box under the "father" title.

It simply said, "Unknown."

I watched him as he scanned the next paper. Andy rubbed his fingers across a small area of the paper, and I wondered what was on it. He had tears in his eyes. After a minute, he handed it to me. It was a copy of a Certificate of Birth, from the hospital where Emma was born.

It had Emma's tiny footprints stamped in ink on it. Andy had been touching the area where her footprints were stamped.

Oh God, her tiny, little footprints.

Suddenly, Andy set everything else aside and got off the bed.

"I need a minute, Zoey," he mumbled as he walked into the bathroom and closed the door.

Within seconds, I heard him sobbing. My heart broke again at the sound, and I began to cry myself.

For several agonizing minutes, I watched his shadow pacing back and forth past the gap between the floor and the door. I knew he was probably touching his face and running his fingers across his stubbly jaw the way he did when he was upset. I wanted to go to him, but he obviously needed to be alone for a few minutes, so I stayed where I was.

After fifteen minutes, he still hadn't come out, so I went to the bathroom door. I knocked lightly. "Andy, are you okay?"

"Yeah." His voice trembled when he spoke.

I heard him turn on the water in the sink.

"I'll be out in a minute."

Again, I began crying at the sound of his tortured voice over the noise of running water. I wanted to be with him to comfort him, but chose to give him space. I went back to the bed and covered up, drying my tears on the sleeve of my nightgown as he came out of the bathroom.

His eyes were now bright blue, but rimmed red from crying. He returned to the bathroom and retrieved a box of tissues. He sat back on the bed, pulled a tissue from the box, and handed it to me, then brushed his thumb over my cheek to help wipe away the remaining tears.

He still worried about taking care of *me* when he was upset. I pressed his hand against my lips and kissed his palm.

"I love you." I held his hand and looked at him through the tears in my eyes.

He wiped his eyes with the back of his other hand. "Thank you, Zoey."

I wasn't sure what he was thanking me for exactly, so I simply nodded. I let go of him, and he picked up the last few papers that were in the envelope. He sighed heavily as he slowly read the first page, handed it to me, then moved on to the second.

I looked at it and found it was a letter from Michelle. To me, whatever the letter said was between him and her, so I set it aside.

As he continued to read, the tension slowly eased from his body. His shoulders relaxed and his breathing slowed down.

She must have told him about how Emma died, and that it had nothing to do with him.

He handed me the other pages as he finished them and I added them to the rest. I was relieved he was sharing everything with me, but I definitely didn't want to read the letter.

The last thing left for him to look at was whatever was inside the smaller envelope.

He pulled the contents out and looked them over, one by one. After setting them down, he covered his face with his hands, and cried.

They were photos of Emma. I was rendered speechless.

His strong shoulders shook as he sat there and cried. All I could do is scoot closer to him, and rub his back while he looked through the photos again. I rested my head on his shoulder and whispered how much I loved him and that I was there for him.

When he was finished with the pictures, he handed them to me.

I carefully looked over each photo. Emma had been an adorable baby, and I immediately saw a resemblance to Andy in the shape of her eyes, the color of her skin. Her dark hair was the color of Michelle's.

I set the pictures down and looked over at him. He was running his hands roughly over his jaw. I didn't try to stop him. If it helped to ease his heartache, then so be it.

He didn't say anything, so I didn't say anything. We sat in silence as I watched the minutes on the clock tick forward. After an hour, I needed to break the silence and finish our conversation.

"Andy, I'm so sorry for all of this. Even if you don't want to be with me anymore, I refuse to let you go through life not knowing what happened to her. There is too much at stake," I said as I thought about our baby girl.

"Zoey stop, please, *never* apologize for this," he said softly.

The way he was staring into my eyes, I knew I had done the right thing for him.

"If it weren't for you, I wouldn't know what happened to my daughter. Did Michelle tell you anything?"

I nodded. "Yes, she did, and I'm so sorry about Emma."

He leaned over and kissed me. "Thank you . . . so much. Zoey, I love you. I don't know how I can ever thank you enough for this."

Chapter Nine

Zoey

I sat on the bed and wondered if I should tell him the rest now, or wait until the next day. If Andy wanted to wait until the next day, I would need to sleep in another room away from him. I hoped he wanted to continue, but I knew better than to push. He was already overwhelmed with me being here, and with all the information about Emma coming to him unexpectedly.

"There is still a lot more I need to tell you. Do you want to wait until tomorrow?"

"It can't get any worse, right?" he asked plainly.

I shook my head. "No, I promise it can only get better."

He kissed me and thanked me again.

"Alright, what else do you have to show me?" he asked as he tipped his head toward the photo album and folder with my medical records.

"Andy, do you still love me?"

"Yes, of course. I never stopped," he answered without hesitation. He reached out and rested his big hand on my cheek; the tips of his fingers edged into my hair "I love you more than anything, Zoey. Even more now after what you've done for me." His hand traveled from my cheek, down my arm to grasp my engagement ring. "For *us*," he whispered.

Content with his answer and the hope that was blooming in my chest, I smiled and entwined my fingers with his. "I have some questions for you. I'm pretty sure you know I want you to just say *yes* to all of them."

He smirked and squeezed my hand. "Hey, no Snow Patrol in the conversation."

"Sorry, but it's totally necessary," I joked.

"Alright then," he said. A hint of light was coming back into his eyes. "Fire away."

I turned my body to face him, sitting cross-legged, the pillow still on my lap.

"Now that you know what happened, will you come home?"

"Yes."

"Will you marry me?"

"Yes."

"Just one more question, then your inquisition is over," I said jokingly. "Will you close your eyes for a minute?"

"Yes," he said. "Wait, was that the question? 'Cause if it was, it kinda sucked." He gave me a quick kiss on the lips.

I smacked his arm. "No smartass, that wasn't the question."

He continued to smile and closed his eyes. I tossed the pillow and the covers aside and straddled his lap.

"Keep your eyes closed," I said as I pulled my nightgown over my head and draped it around the back of his neck.

He raised his eyebrows. "Are you going to dance for me, Zoey?" He slid his palms up my thighs to rest on my hips.

I couldn't help but laugh. "Um no, not right now . . . but I am sure you could convince me to later."

I had tossed a couple sexy outfits in my luggage, just in case.

He sighed. "What's the last question?"

"Do you still want a baby with me by the time you turn thirty?" I asked hesitantly.

"Yes."

"Good answer."

Taking his hands from my hips, I slid them up my sides and across my belly. He flinched a bit but didn't open his eyes. I moved his big, warm hands around on my stomach, so he could feel the roundness of it beneath his palms. His eyes blinked open when he realized what I was trying to show him. He looked at his hands on my stomach and froze.

"Zoey?" His questioning eyes met mine.

I nodded, letting him know what he was seeing and touching was real.

The next several seconds, were complete confusion for him. He mumbled incoherently through the enormous grin on his face. The only words I understood were how, what, and when as he stared at my body in awe.

I couldn't help but laugh. It was adorable. He was in complete shock.

The next thing I knew, he was pulling me into his arms, and again, he was crying. That of course, made me cry too.

He was thrilled, and it made me happy.

After a few minutes, we finally pulled apart so he could look at me again.

"Can I put my pajamas back on?" I took my nightgown from the back of his neck.

He nodded, still obviously in shock.

I slipped it back over my head and he immediately pushed it back up over my stomach so he could touch it again.

He wiped his eyes and smiled up at me. "If you're finished with your questions, I think you have some explaining to do about this."

Where do I begin? "I'm eighteen weeks along," I started.

"Eighteen weeks?" he asked in disbelief, his brows furrowed. "How long have you known?"

I became a little worried at the tone of his voice. "I've known a month. I'm so sorry I didn't tell you sooner, but I needed to make sure everything was okay first . . . and I didn't think it was right for me to tell you over the phone."

He nodded. "Go on." He rested his hands on me again. A grin slowly eased over his face, and tears pooled in his blue eyes.

"Do you remember back in May when I switched pills?"

He nodded, not looking away from where his hands rested on my stomach.

"Remember how sick I was with the flu around that time?"

Again, he nodded.

I was beginning to wonder if he would ever speak again.

"Well, apparently throwing up for four days straight didn't allow my body to absorb my birth control pills."

He smiled and shook his head, still touching my stomach. He was in utter disbelief. It was endearing. I laughed nervously, knowing the next thing I needed to tell him was the *where* portion of the story.

"Do you remember the first night of the drags, and how I helped you with your car trailer when we got home?"

His eyes darted back up to mine when he figured out what I was telling him.

"Seriously?" He began laughing right along with me. Andy took his hands from my belly and covered his face with them for just a moment. He wore a proud grin on his face and shook his head while laughing.

"Yeah, baby . . . pretty sure you knocked me up on the hood of your car."

He laughed harder. "Please tell me we are the only people who know about that part."

I nodded. "Yep, just us, and I plan on keeping it that way."

He kissed me. "Thank you. Just what I need is for your dad and brothers to find out about that part and beat my ass. So what else do you have to show me?" he asked as he patted the photo album.

After leaving his lap, I sat next to him and handed him the album. He looked through the pictures I'd arranged in it. When he reached the sonogram pictures, he was awestruck. "This is incredible, Zoey." He traced the shape of our baby in the photo with his fingertip then set the album aside. He picked up the folder with my medical records and flipped it open.

"What are these for?"

"Well," I said, dragging the word out. "Depending on how long we're going to stay here, I might need to see a doctor. Those are my medical records."

He looked at me, surprised. "You want to stay here, in En Zed?"

"I want to be wherever you are, Andy. If you want to live here, I'm fine with that. I bought a one-way ticket, just in case."

He shook his head. "No, we belong in Sacramento, with the rest of our family. You can't give up everything you've worked so hard for, Zoey. Not for me . . . I won't let you do it."

With a nod of agreement, I burrowed down in the bed and curled up next to him, resting my arm over his stomach. I was happy and relieved that he wanted to go back to Sacramento.

"Are you tired?" he asked.

I nodded. "It's been a long month."

He gathered everything from the bed, took it over to his dresser, and set it down.

"Can you get your laptop for me?" I wanted to show him one more thing that I knew he would love to see.

He brought it over from the closet and powered it on.

I found my purse and dug the DVD's of my sonogram out of it.

"I have another surprise for you." I slid the DVD into the drive. "Unless you've had enough surprises for the day?"

"Nah, I'm intrigued now," he said as he looked at the screen.

"I didn't want you to miss anything," I said as the DVD began to play.

We watched as our baby bounced around on the screen.

"I can't believe this is happening, Zoey."

I knotted my fingers with his and kissed the back of his hand. "Do you want to know if we're having a boy or girl?"

"Do you know already?" he asked excitedly.

I nodded.

"Then I want to know too."

"We're having a girl."

His face lit up as he smiled and rubbed my belly again. "A sweet, baby girl," he whispered.

"So, Andy . . . I noticed on my tour of the house earlier today that your old bedroom is a little . . . *black*."

He raised his eyebrows when he looked away from my stomach and back up to my eyes. "And?" He smirked.

I picked the bag up from the floor on my side of the bed and handed it to him. "I know we're having a little girl, but I think she'll look adorable in all black." Yes, I was using Iria's pun. It was hilarious.

He grinned as he pulled the items from my shopping spree at Champions of the World out of the bag and looked them over. The baby clothes were so tiny compared to his large hands.

"Thank you. Can I teach her to play rugby?" He was still grinning from ear to ear.

I could only think of one answer. "Yes."

After he set aside the clothes and his laptop, he shut off the lights, stripped his clothes off, and crawled into bed with me.

"Can we practice making baby number two now?" He laughed as he gently pushed me back on the bed.

I definitely knew the answer to that question.

Hell yes!

Andy

Heaven . . . I had died and gone to heaven. There was no other explanation for it. I'd gone from being a depressed coward that morning, to feeling like I was on top of the world. Zoey slept soundly in my arms, hogging the bed the way she usually did. Technically, she didn't hog the bed, she hogged me. And I would never tire of it. She slept wrapped around me, the slight swell of our baby nestled protectively between us.

After making love to her, she had curled up against me and dozed off. I was too excited about her being here to sleep. Emma was also weighing heavily on my mind. Reading the letter from Michelle and seeing the photos of Emma just about killed me. Especially the one of Michelle holding her, wrapped in a hospital blanket. I was angry, sad, and resentful that she had held her, when I had never even known she'd existed.

But then Zoey took care of me when I needed her the most. Even after what I'd done to her, she never wavered once while I went through the contents of the envelope Michelle had sent. She wrapped her arms around me when I needed it. Then she checked in on me when I couldn't bring myself to come out of the bathroom. I didn't want to upset her because I couldn't hold back the tears. She let me sit and absorb everything, and it was exactly what I'd needed.

And the way she gave me the news that she was pregnant . . . it was pure Zoey. And I was the luckiest bastard alive to have her. I thought it might sting a bit when she said we were having a baby girl, because of Emma, but it didn't. Even though I never saw Emma, she couldn't be replaced by mine and Zoey's child.

No matter what happened the next day, I was going to relish the fact that my beautiful Zoey had accomplished everything I should have done myself. She had brought me answers. She brought my life back to me and we had unexpectedly made a life together.

A baby. I was going to be a dad and Zoey a perfect mum. I was going to give her the world after what she'd given me.

Chapter Ten

Zoey

The next morning, I sat on the edge of the bathtub in Andy's bathroom drying my tears and gathering my composure so I could go back to the bedroom. After eventually getting over the initial shock of him leaving in August, I had allowed myself only twenty minutes a day to mourn the loss of him and our relationship.

If I hadn't given myself time each day, I would have slipped back in to the depression that I'd fought so hard to overcome. I had struggled daily to keep myself motivated to do everything I needed to get him back, but I had also needed to grieve. He had broken my heart when he left. Knowing his child was growing safely inside me, was the only thing that had kept me sane without him.

Now that we were back together, I was letting myself cry over the fact that all of my plans had worked and everything was out in the open.

Still naked from the night before, I quietly stepped out of the bathroom. Andy was sprawled across the bed on his stomach, his right leg hanging off the bed from the knee down. The white sheet was barely covering his gorgeous, naked body.

I loved the way he slept. Always as if he fell face first on the bed. I thought it was amusing that anyone could sleep like that. It was crazy, but I missed watching him sleep, so I stood silently and gazed down at my beautiful man.

At first glance, I thought he had lost weight since the last time I saw him. But as I watched him sleep, I realized he'd been playing so much rugby since he'd been back, his body was more toned than before. I thought back to when I watched him play rugby on the way to his house and realized most of the other guys playing also had similar forms. Strong thighs, round muscular asses, trim waists, and well-built shoulders and arms.

A rugby player's body.

I pulled the sheet off him to admire him further. I didn't think his butt could get any more attractive, but it had from all that running.

Enduring over a month of not touching him made me anxious to make up for lost time.

Giggling quietly, I knelt on the floor next to where his leg was hanging off the bed and kissed the arch on the bottom of his foot. I made my way up the back of his leg slowly, kissing and gently biting his gorgeous, golden skin every few inches.

He was stirring when I made it to the back of his thigh. I decided to take it a bit further when I arrived at that ass of his. I lightly bit down on the center of his right cheek.

Yep, smooth and firm. Exactly what I suspected.

He raised his head and sleepily looked over his shoulder at me as I hovered over him with a mischievous smile on my face.

"Zoey, did you just *bite* my ass cheek?"

"Yep," I said honestly. "And you better lie still 'cause I'm gonna bite the other side right now." So I did.

He groaned as I kissed his lower back, then kissed, and licked all the way up his spine causing goose bumps to break out over his tattooed skin. I placed a kiss on each letter of my name that he had inked on his side.

Once I began kissing across his shoulder, he slowly rolled over onto his back. His rock hard erection was pressing right where I needed it to. I slipped my hand down in between us and eased him slowly inside me.

"Good morning, my love," I whispered into his ear right before I lightly bit his earlobe.

His hands roamed up my thighs to my waist as he rotated his hips upward, pushing himself the rest of the way inside me.

"I've missed you," he mumbled into my ear. "I'm so sorry for leaving—"

I kissed him so he'd stop talking.

"Later . . ." I murmured as I sat up and rested my hands behind me on his thighs as he rocked me back and forth.

Andy sat up, pulling my legs around him. My arms instinctively went around his neck and I wound my fingers in his hair. It had grown out quite a bit since he'd left, so I actually had something to grab on to this time.

We sat motionless, clinging to each other, letting the time and space between us reunite our hearts.

After a few minutes, we moved together in a slow, torturous rhythm, his face buried in the side of my neck, his lips, tongue, and teeth teasing me endlessly. He untangled my arms from around his neck and pulled back to kiss and lick his way to my breasts. He took his time to tease and torture me until my body was clenching around him. Then he took my legs from around his waist, and laid me back on the bed. He slowly pulled out of me, the emptiness making me long for him to fill me again.

On his hands and knees, he hovered over me. He kissed my forehead, the tip of my nose, each cheek, and my chin before moving on to my lips.

"I love you, Zoey," he whispered in between each kiss. He nipped my bottom lip, and sucked it lightly into his mouth before he slid his warm, wet tongue inside to meet mine.

We stayed there kissing, hands roaming, for what seemed like an eternity, before he made his way down my neck to my breasts again. He licked and sucked them as he teased me with his fingers, until I was panting for more.

He brought his face back up to mine and guided my arms around his neck. Reaching down in between us, he slipped himself back inside me. Pushing my legs upward, he rested the backs of my knees in the crook of his elbows.

His big hands cradling my ass, he picked me up, until he was on his knees in the center of the bed, my back pressed against the soft, cushioned headboard.

"Hold on tight," he groaned as he pushed all the way inside me.

"I'm too heavy now." I gasped as he began moving against me.

"No, Beautiful . . . I've got you. I'll always have you," he said quietly.

He groaned as he rocked his hips back and gripped my hips and ass with his large hands. He slowly pulled me to him as he ground himself against me. *Holy hell.*

He continued the slow, agonizing torture of my body until it trembled then he laid me back on the bed.

"You're so beautiful, Zoey," he said as he hovered over me and gently thrust himself inside me. He covered my body with his and whispered, "I love you so much and I'm so sorry for leaving. Please forgive me."

"I forgive you," I whispered to him as I looked into his blue eyes. I gripped his ass as I wrapped my legs around the backs of his thighs and pulled him into me.

He began thrusting, propped up on one elbow to keep most of his weight off me. His other hand was gently cupping my face as he kissed me.

He was slowly torturing me, and I craved my release. Now.

"Please, Andy . . . I need you." I moaned as I dug my nails into his back, knowing it would set him off.

"Ahh, fuck. You feel amazing Zoey," he groaned as he picked up his pace and rotated his hips against me.

That's what I needed to feel, right there.

"Again . . ." I sighed, my breath catching.

Every nerve ending in my body was buzzing. I dragged my nails down his back slowly.

He thrust faster.

My hands gripped his ass again. I dug my nails in and ran them up his back, leaving him shivering in their wake.

He ground his hips and slammed into me one last time, before I came hard around him. His own orgasm ripped through him at the same time as mine.

"Oh Zoey . . . fuck, I can't take it when you do that."

When we were both completely spent, he slowly pulled out of me and kissed me.

The next thing I knew, he was jumping off me and freaking out.

"What the fuck did I just do?" he bellowed as he dropped to his knees beside the bed and ran his hands over my belly. "Are you okay?" he asked, looking first at me, then at my stomach again. "Did I hurt you? Was I too rough? Shit, I'm so sorry."

He was so frantic, for a split second I thought he might need to be slapped like they did in the movies when someone was having an epic freak out. Not that I would ever slap him, but he was worrying me because he wouldn't calm down.

I grabbed his face in my hands to get his attention back on me. "Hey, Sexy, I am fine. Chill out."

He stopped freaking out and his eyes met mine. "Are you sure?"

I nodded and pointed at myself. "Totally fine here. I'll tell you if you are too rough, I promise."

He finally seemed convinced. "I love you." He stood and kissed me on the head. "I'll go start you a bath." And he was back in "take care of Zoey" mode. After he returned from the bathroom, he pulled on his shorts that were lying on the floor next to the bed.

"I'll give you some time alone, and I'll go find us something for brekkie."

I smiled at his word for breakfast as he turned and shut the door behind him.

Seeing steam billowing from the tub, I turned down the temperature on the water so I could get in. He knew I loved hot baths, but since I was pregnant, I had to ease up quite a bit on the temperature. Once the too hot water was cool enough for me, I lowered myself into it, submerging my body and head.

I wondered if this was how our baby felt floating around inside me.

Needing to breathe, I emerged and wiped the water from my eyes before reclining against the back of the tub. I watched the rain outside hit the windows and slowly drip down the glass, while the trees closest to the house swayed from the light breeze.

Since I was alone and away from Andy, everything that happened over the last month and a half was sinking in. I had finally found a chance to relax and think about myself for a minute. How the hell had I made it through all of that? Especially without Andy with me. He had been my rock for months, and then he'd been gone.

I knew if I weren't pregnant, things would have surely been different. I wouldn't be in this picturesque country, with my beautiful man.

But, I had been given something so much bigger than myself, and my own life to take care of. She was part of me, and part of Andy, and I loved her more than life. She had needed me to get him back, for us both.

Almost as if she knew what I was feeling, our little girl moved inside me. I set my hands on my stomach and gently massaged over my skin. I wondered whom she would look like when she was born. Would she look like me? What traits of Andy's would she get?

I thought back to what my birth mother looked like. She had been pretty once, before drugs took her to the point of no return. The last time I had seen her, she'd been almost skeletal, with sores all over her body, and she had been missing most of her teeth from the use of meth. What teeth she had left, had been black and rotten.

I had no idea what my birth father, or what anyone else in my family looked like. Were any of them decent people? Did I have siblings out there somewhere? Did they know about me? If I did have any natural family out there and they knew of my mother's drug habit, why hadn't they helped me? Why hadn't they done something?

I decided then, I was not going to try and find out. Now I have my amazing parents, four overprotective brothers, Andy, and my wonderful friends. *They* were my true family.

Once our daughter was born, I'd have my own little family.

I wasn't sure what she would inherit from me, but I knew I loved her more than life the second I found out I was pregnant. And the fact that she was part of Andy too— the person I loved most in my life, until her—made me feel like my life was exactly as it should be.

As parents, we would give our daughter everything she could ever need.

From Andy, she would get what he had as a child. A loving family who took care of each other, cherished each other, and loved each other unconditionally.

I wondered what I had to offer her. She would definitely get more love, affection, and protection from me, than I ever received from my mother.

She would be beautiful, inside and out, without a doubt.

I slipped back under the water to wash, then stepped carefully out of the slick-bottomed tub and dried off. I dressed then stood in front of the mirror, my eyes wandering over my body as I took in the new fullness of my breasts, and the roundness of my abdomen. Even with clothes covering me, I could tell I was different. I had changed so much physically over the last month and a half.

Had I changed emotionally too? I felt stronger than I had in years, but I still struggled. I still fought my insecurities, and probably always would.

One thing was for sure, I would do anything to protect my little family.

As I ran my comb through my wet hair, I sung quietly to myself. Noticing a movement behind me, I looked up in the mirror and found Andy watching me from the doorway.

He came to stand behind me and put his arms around me, resting his big hands on our baby.

"What are you singing, Zoey?"

"'Beautiful With You,' by Halestorm."

"I like it," he said against my neck.

"It's the way you make me feel," I said quietly. "You see me for who I am and accept me."

"Because I love you. You can't imagine how much I've missed hearing you sing." He moved his hands around on me. "I hope she gets your voice."

"Thank you, but I seem to remember that you can sing too. Either way, I think she'll sing."

I thought back to my concerns about my birth mom and turned to Andy, hugging him tight for comfort.

"Hey, what's wrong?" He returned my embrace.

"What if I'm like my birth mom?" I choked back tears. "What if I mess up and our daughter turns out fucked up like me? Oh God . . . I can't be like her."

He took my shoulders firmly and held me at arm's length.

"Zoey, no," he said adamantly, staring into my eyes. "Do you have any idea how strong you are? She was weak and selfish. Those are two things you definitely are *not*. Look at everything you've done in the last several weeks. You put our daughter first."

"I just wanted you to come back to me. How is that putting her first?"

He shook his head swiftly from side to side.

"It's putting her first because you went and saw Michelle to make sure she would be healthy. You've been through hell the last six weeks. You put me before yourself too, for that matter. *You* went out and found the answers *I* needed, while I took the coward's way out and left the fucking country."

He let go of me and slowly ran his hands through his hair, then down his jaw line. A fresh wave of guilt washed over his face, causing his blue eyes to be stricken with grief and tears.

Oh how I wished I never called him a coward before he left for New Zealand.

"I'm so sorry for saying that." I took his hands in mine as tears spilled from my eyes. "Andy, I didn't mean it . . . I was so furious with you. Please, I *need* you to forgive me. I shouldn't have said it and I wish I could take it back. Please let me take it back . . ."

He dropped to his knees in front of me and rested his forehead on my belly. His hands gripped my hips tightly.

"You were right though, Zoey. I'll forgive you for saying it, if it's what you need me to do, but it's true. I deserved it. I'm a coward and what I did to you is unforgivable. I'm sorry for putting you through hell."

Taking his stubbly face in my hands, I tilted his head up so he had to look at me. "I've already forgiven you. I know it will never happen again."

He shook his head, tears still in his guilt-ridden eyes. "No, it won't. I'll never leave you again, Zoey. I made a huge mistake before. Since the day I left, I wanted to come home, but I didn't know how to fix everything. I didn't know how to make it right. But you did it for me. You did it for us, and you'll never have to worry again."

He lifted my shirt up just enough to press his lips to the bare flesh surrounding our child.

"Hey, baby girl," he said to my belly as he rubbed his palms over it. "You don't know who I am yet, but I'm your daddy. I love you so much already."

I loved the fact he was using the nickname my dad used with me, on our daughter.

Tears flowed freely down my face and I didn't bother trying to wipe them away. I rested my hands on his shoulders while he knelt in front of me talking to our little girl. Once again, she was fluttering around inside me, reacting to his voice.

"She already knows you . . ." I whispered to Andy when he glanced up at me for a brief second.

He looked back to my stomach. "Your mum has taken such good care of you, but now I'm here to take care of you both. I'm not going anywhere."

He looked back up at me, his eyes pleading with mine, and tears rolled down his face. "Zoey, I'm not going anywhere," he whispered.

I nodded, and wiped the moisture from his cheeks. I couldn't speak, and I couldn't bear to see him cry.

He kissed my stomach again. "I love you, baby girl."

He stood and pulled me into his arms. His body vibrated with emotion. "I love you, Zoey. Thank you for everything you've done, for coming here . . . For giving me everything I've ever wanted. You two are my life. Will you marry me? Here, in En Zed? I want to be your husband right away. I can't go another day without you . . . and without *her*."

"Yes, I will." I would never tell him no, and would marry him anywhere in the world he wanted.

We stood holding each other, letting our emotional conversation fade away.

"I think she heard you, Andy. While you were talking to her and touching me, she was moving."

He looked at me, his eyes full of wonder and excitement. "She was?"

I loved seeing the expression on his face. I smiled. "Try it again."

He knelt down, rested his palms on me, and he talked to her again. Telling her how pretty she was going to be, but that she was going to be tough too. He told her about how he was going to teach her to play rugby, and how her *mum* was going to teach her to sing.

He looked up at me inquisitively.

"She's in there bouncing all over the place."

"I better go make something to feed your mum, baby girl. You're probably hungry too." He kissed my belly again and stood.

"Are we going to be okay Zoey?"

"Yes."

He grinned and kissed me.

Chapter Eleven

Zoey

"Guess what I found while you were in the bath earlier?" Andy asked when we arrived in the kitchen.

"I have no clue, what did you find?"

"A note from Iria and Tamati saying they are spending the next two weeks with Tamati's family. They want to give us some time . . . so we have the whole house to ourselves."

"Wow, that's an unexpected surprise. Iria didn't mention that while we were making plans for me to come here." That definitely made things easier for us to have private conversations and spend quality time together.

As we ate the breakfast he'd cooked, he kept sneaking extra food onto my plate, thinking I didn't notice. I'd sneak it back onto his plate when he would look away. I told him about Adam teasing me for getting seconds at dinner, before I found out I was pregnant, and how I flung an entire serving spoon full of beans all over him for payback.

"That's my girl," he said as he high-fived me.

After breakfast, we went back upstairs to his room where I laid down on the bed to read while Andy showered and dressed. Once he was finished, he curled up on his side next to me and I played with his hair.

"What do you feel like doing today?" I asked.

He fiddled around with my engagement ring and kept his eyes transfixed on it before he gave me an answer I never expected.

"Can we go to the cemetery?"

The shock of his question took my breath away, but there was no way I would deny him. "Absolutely." I quickly shut off my Kindle. He was taking me to his family. We gathered our rain jackets and rain boots, and he drove us to where his parents and sister were buried.

The minute we arrived, I forced myself to hold back the tears that were pooling in my eyes.

This was huge for him, with me being here, and I needed to be strong . . . *for him.*

When he stepped out of the car, I quickly pulled myself together. He opened the back door to get our boots and jackets out, and then came around to my side of the car to help me into mine.

I held his hand as we wound our way through the cemetery. He'd been here so many times he found their plots easily. There were fresh flowers in granite vases next to each one. He took a few minutes and knelt down to straighten flowers, while I read the names and dates on the beautiful, black granite headstones. Each headstone had a fern leaf etched into it, along with the names of Andy's family.

Callum, Katherine, and Hannah Tate. All lost, March 10th, 2001.

His sister had been only twelve years old when she died.

He stood and took my hand in his.

I held it tightly and leaned into him. I wasn't sure if I was comforting him or me.

"Mum, Dad, Hannah, this is my beautiful fiancée, Zoey." He looked down at the headstones.

There was nothing but love in his eyes. I gently squeezed his hand and wiped my eyes. As sad as I was for Andy, when I looked at him, he was smiling. It seemed to be a happy smile even, as if he were actually introducing me to them.

"We're having a baby. A girl," he said at last, as he placed his hand over our baby girl.

My hand automatically covered his, joining the three of us together.

He pulled me close, wrapped his arm around my shoulder, and squeezed. "Everything is finally right in my life. We're moving back to Sacramento soon to raise our daughter, and be near Zoey's family . . . *our* family."

I squeezed him a little tighter when he said that.

"I also found out I have another daughter. Her name is Emma. I'm sorry I didn't tell you sooner, but I didn't know what happened to her until Zoey came here. Emma is there with you. I hope you can find her and take care of her until I get there. I miss you all, so much."

Hearing him ask that of his family made me physically ill. My body tightened in anguish from the top of my head, to the tips of my toes and I felt my heart sink to my stomach at the thought of him dying. My eyes filled with tears again when he told them how much he missed them.

God, what he must have gone through when they died. I couldn't even imagine. Unable to hold back the tears anymore, I let them flow freely down my face. There was no point in keeping them from falling.

"Don't cry, Beautiful. I've waited a long time for this day. Thank you for coming here with me and for coming to En Zed." He wiped my tears away with his fingers.

Once he cleared the tears from my face, I turned to him and slipped my arms inside his jacket, and pressed my cheek to his chest, just over his heart. The steady thump against my face reminded me just how much life we still had ahead of us. I stood on my toes to reach his mouth, pressing a kiss to his lips before we said our goodbyes to his family, and slowly walked back to the car.

After tossing my jacket onto the backseat, I sat on the passenger seat and Andy knelt to pull off my rain boots. I raised my hand to his cheek and slowly rubbed my thumb back and forth to get his attention. I had a very important question to ask him.

"Can we name our daughter Hannah, after your sister?" I asked when his blue eyes finally met mine.

He smiled as his eyes filled with tears. "Yes Zoey, thank you. I love that idea."

Andy leaned into the car, wrapped his arms around me, and his entire body shook with emotion.

Every time he cried, it felt like my heart was being ripped from my chest. I hated seeing him so distraught.

After we returned to his house, we followed the path to the beach. We walked in silence across the sand before he finally spoke. "Do you think tomorrow we might go a day without crying?"

I wasn't sure if he was joking or not, but I could tell it bothered him.

"I'll try," I said hesitantly. "These pregnancy hormones are kind of scary sometimes, so no promises."

We continued down the beach.

"Andy, you know crying doesn't make you weak or anything, right?"

He draped his arm over my shoulders and I reached up to lace my fingers with his.

"I know. I just feel like all I've been doing the last month and a half is crying or being so angry I can't even see straight." He stopped walking and turned to face me. "Then out of the blue, you're here . . . And you've set everything right. You completely blindsided me, and for the second time in my life, it's been in a *good* way. You've done it both times. You're my good luck charm, Zoey."

I kissed his hand. "And you're mine."

While we were here, we needed to talk about his family because after talking to his Aunt Sarah, I knew he hadn't been able to grieve for them properly. We continued our walk along the beach and I wondered how to approach the subject carefully. I wanted to help him find the closure I felt he so desperately needed.

But, I needed him to see it and be willing to help himself.

"How long did you live here after your parents and sister died?"

"It wasn't long at all," he replied. "Maybe two months, why?"

I thought about my words wisely before I spoke them. "Do you think you had enough time to grieve for them?"

He looked at me curiously.

"What I mean is . . ." How could I say what I needed to without him taking it the wrong way? "Okay, look, I didn't know anyone in my family except my mother. I spent years in therapy after I was adopted trying to get rid of all the blame I placed on myself for her doing the things she did. I thought that maybe if I'd been a better kid, she wouldn't have needed to do drugs or prostitute herself out to disgusting men—"

"She was a prostitute? You never told me that." Andy stopped abruptly and stared down at me.

I could see the confusion in his eyes from my choice of words.

"She wasn't a normal prostitute, at least not in the usual sense of the word."

I held in a chuckle at my use of the term "normal prostitute" so I wouldn't freak Andy out. He still looked confused though.

"She wasn't the standing-on-a-street-corner-with-a-pimp kind of prostitute. She had certain men she would *see,* and in return, they would keep her supplied with meth."

He nodded in understanding and we began walking again.

"I've gotten completely off the subject now." I laughed.

"How can you laugh?" he asked.

"I can laugh because I've dealt with that part of my life. The blame I put on myself for the crap she did—it wasn't right. It wasn't my blame or guilt to carry."

This time I abruptly stopped walking. I needed to steer the conversation back to him.

"I think . . . that in a way, you are either putting blame on yourself for the accident, or you haven't really dealt with it at all. I'm guessing it's a little of both."

He seemed to comprehend what I was trying to say.

"I know you've been to the cemetery, but have you been to the place where the accident happened?"

He cringed and took a small step backward. I knew at that very second, I'd hit a nerve.

"No."

In all the months we had known each other, every time we'd talk about his family, he'd be brief and almost nonchalant about everything. He glossed over their story and moved on to a different subject.

On occasion, he let his guard down and shared memories, but those times were few, and far between.

"Will you go there with me, please?" I closed the distance between us.

He clenched his jaw and shook his head. "I can't Zoey."

"Yes, you can." I took his hands and placed them on my belly because I felt *she* might put everything in to perspective for him like she had so often for me. "This is exactly why you need to go, Andy."

He looked away from me and shook his head again. I stared at the man who had been so strong when he helped me get myself back together. The man who stood in front of me now was broken and battered by life the way I had once been. He desperately needed my help, and I hoped he would realize it.

"Hey," I said quietly. "Look at me, please."

His uncertain eyes met mine.

I was getting to him.

"I think if you go, you'll see how everything that happened there has brought you to this point in your life. I know you wish it would've never happened, but it did. You survived the crash for a reason. And the reason—*both* of them—are standing right here in front of you."

I took a breath and watched for his reaction.

He still didn't speak.

"You deserved a second chance. I needed another chance . . . you came into my life when I needed you most. Sure, things haven't gone smoothly the whole time, but . . . here we are. We need to do this for us, and for *Hannah*."

It was a dirty trick to use his sister and our daughter's name against him, but I didn't know how else to get through to him. He really needed to go to where the accident had happened. Just like I had faced my fears and my past so many months ago. I had chosen to help myself, but it was because of him, that I was able to make that decision. It was finally his chance to do the same for himself, with a little nudge from me. He was my *reason,* and he always would be.

He needed me to help him now . . . to be *his* reason.

"I haven't been back there, Zoey," he said quietly. "Not since that night. I didn't even go back to school afterward."

I took his hand and started walking back to his house.

"Then that's what we need to do. We can go together." He needed to know I would be there for him.

Neither of us spoke on our stroll back. We went inside and I sat him down at the table in the kitchen and prepared our lunch. I was giving him time to think about what I said.

We finished eating, and I washed our lunch dishes while he continued to sit at the table. As I stood in front of the sink, staring out the window, he came up behind me and rested his chin on my shoulder.

"I'll do it," he said softly.

I turned and kissed him on the lips. "Let's go then."

We needed to leave before he changed his mind.

As I drove to the last place I saw my family alive, Zoey kept my mood light and joked with me about how driving in New Zealand was driving on the wrong side of the road, and how the steering wheel was on the wrong side of the car. I joked back with her by asking how it could be wrong, when the steering wheel was on the right side of the car, *literally*.

That meant it was right. *Right?*

She politely refused my offer to teach her how to drive in New Zealand. It was second nature to me, so she was more than fine with me driving us anywhere we needed to go.

On the way, I played tour guide and pointed out several buildings to her. We passed a building where I went to school as a boy, a house where one of my friends used to live. As we drove, the houses and buildings were becoming further apart, which meant we were getting close. We eventually came to the long, straight stretch in the road where the accident had happened.

Off in the distance, I saw my old school and the small sports arena where I had played rugby.

I eased up on my grip of the steering wheel when I realized I was holding it so tightly my knuckles had turned white. That was when I noticed we were quickly approaching our destination. I abruptly pulled off the road and stopped the car.

"This is it," I said quietly, staring down at the steering wheel. Pulling in a deep, shaky breath, I glanced up and pointed at my old school. "The building over there—that's where I went to school, and I had a rugby game that night. Coach sent me to the sin bin for punching another player because he kicked me in the face while we were on the ground. Fights were a common occurrence when we played against each other."

I absentmindedly touched the scar on my nose from where his boot had connected that night. Every day when I looked into the mirror, I was reminded of all I'd lost. It was a horrible daily reminder.

Zoey took my hand in hers, giving it an encouraging squeeze.

"Once I'd showered and dressed after the game, Coach pulled me aside to talk to me about it. I only talked to him for twenty minutes, but those twenty minutes had us running later than usual. We were supposed to meet Hamish and Sarah for dinner, so my dad was in a rush to get to the restaurant. The weather was horrible that night. It was dark, and the roads were slick from the rain. I saw the headlights of the truck coming toward us, and at the last second, it swerved and hit our car."

After taking several deep breaths, I got out of the car and sat on the hood.

Zoey followed and her eyes scanned the area.

"Our car came to a stop out there," I said and pointed past where she was standing.

Suddenly, she spun and walked down the small hill toward the spot where our car came to rest that fateful night.

My heart thudded in my chest and I felt the nausea rolling in my stomach. I didn't want her to be where my family had died.

"Zoey, don't go out there, *please*," I pleaded.

She kept walking and finally stopped. Circling around to face me, she held her hand out to me, beckoning me to her. "Is this the spot, right here?"

Nodding a response, I raised my hands to run them over my face, but halfway there I stopped. If Zoey was strong enough to do everything she'd done to overcome her past, then I could too. I lowered my hands and rested them on my knees.

"Please come out here and be with us." Zoey continued to hold her hand out to me. She rested the palm of her other hand on our growing baby.

After hesitating, I finally stood and slowly walked over to her. When I reached her side, I told her what I remembered. "The truck was going so fast, and hit us so hard it took hours to get my dad and Hannah out. My mum sat in front of me, and her seat was pushed back against my legs. They had to get her out, and remove her seat, before they could get me out to take me to the hospital. I had to sit in the car with my family around me . . . all dead."

"Jesus."

She whispered so softly I barely heard her. I slipped my arms around her for comfort, and knew that coming out here would help. "I was going in and out of consciousness most of the time, so I don't remember much. Just flashes of memories here and there, and then whatever I was told later by other people." I placed my palms on her perfect belly. "I didn't want to do this, Beautiful . . . but now that we're here, I know it was the right thing to do."

"Andy, we can go now, but I think while we're still in New Zealand, we should come back out here. This will give you a push in the right direction to heal. You can even go without me if you want to."

I nodded. "Yeah, being out here will help me. But I always want you with me."

She hugged my neck and kissed me sweetly. "I'll always be wherever you are if you need me to be, but sometimes I think you should come alone. I understand if you need to lean on me at times, but coming here by yourself will help you face your losses and grow stronger. We can stay here in New Zealand as long as you need to."

God, she was so fucking smart and knew exactly what to say and do for me. I was the luckiest man in the world to have her by my side again.

Chapter Twelve

Zoey

Monday morning, we drove to the Auckland courthouse and filled out all the necessary paperwork to get married. There, we set the date and time for our wedding. We would be getting married on the beach in front of Andy's house the following week. From the courthouse, we went to the mall to shop for our wedding clothes.

We were getting something casual to wear since it would be only us, with Iria and Tamati as our witnesses, but still I wanted a beautiful dress for the occasion. It was, after all, our wedding. We also split up because I didn't want him to see what I was going to be wearing.

After I bought my dress and veil, I stepped into a store and found a display of Greenstone jewelry. All of the pieces were so unique and from what I knew, the stone was only found in New Zealand. The accessories would fit perfectly with my dress and veil.

Scanning the glass case, I was having a hard time deciding which pendant to buy for my necklace.

"You should get that one."

I jumped when Andy spoke. I was concentrating so hard I had no idea he was next to me, or how long he had been standing there.

He tapped on the glass over a pendant shaped in a traditional Maori double twist style.

I glanced over at him. "Do you like that one?"

"Yes. It represents the joining of two people for eternity."

I smiled and melted into his embrace as he put his arm around me.

"I'd say it's the one for me then." Next to that pendant, I saw one similar that had three twists, instead of two. "Does the triple twist have the same meaning as the double?"

He nodded.

"I want the triple instead, to represent us, and Hannah. She is a part of us after all, and she will be there when we get married."

Andy smiled down at me. "That's brilliant, Zoey." He tangled his fingers in my hair and kissed my forehead.

The salesperson came over to help us. I chose a thin, black cord for the pendant and then found a Greenstone bracelet that I loved as well.

And just like when we were in Mexico, he slipped his credit card to the cashier before I could get my wallet out, and bought my jewelry for me.

"I could've paid for that, you know?" I said to him as we left the store.

"We're going to be married at the end of next week. You ought to get used to the fact that everything I own, is now yours." He smiled as he laced his fingers through mine. "And I'd like to buy my amazingly perfect fiancée some jewelry."

I scrunched my nose up at him. "I guess that's something we'll need to talk about, isn't it?"

"We'll make everything legal with the house and . . . other things before we go back to Sacramento."

"What do you mean?" I asked. "And, by the way, you never told me you *owned* a house."

He stopped abruptly and looked down at me. "I didn't?"

"Um, no . . . you didn't."

He frowned. "Yeah, we'll definitely need to talk about it . . . later though."

What did he mean by that? He began walking again, but when I didn't follow, he came back.

"I want to make sure that legally, you and I own the house. *Together*," he clarified.

I was still staring at him trying to figure out what the hell was going on, and why he was so adamant about it.

"Zoey, the house is paid off. Everything I own is paid for. Don't worry about it." His eyebrows furrowed. "Are you *sure* I didn't tell you about the house? I swear I did."

I thought about it briefly, and vaguely remembered a conversation when he'd told me about his six-month long trip to New Zealand after his divorce. *What did he say exactly?*

The conversation came back to me in bits and pieces.

"Andy, you did tell me about your place. I'm sorry, I can't remember your exact words, but you said something about a house that your friends rented. I think I misunderstood though, when you told me."

He nodded and bent to kiss me. "Can we go buy our wedding rings now?" After I agreed, he led me straight out the doors of the mall and into the parking garage, or the "car park" as he referred to it.

"Um, where are we going?"

"We're going to buy wedding rings." He smirked then gave me an adorable grin.

Duh Zoey. "What's wrong with the jewelry store at the mall?"

He just smiled. "They don't have the ring I want to buy you there."

Mmmkay . . .

He drove through Auckland and eventually pulled up in front of a Tiffany & Co. store.

Seriously? Did every country have one of these stores?

I winced as I read the sign on the front of the building.

"What's wrong?" he asked.

"Andy, I know how much money you spent on my engagement ring since you left the receipt at my apartment." I said it quickly, to get it all out, like ripping off a freaking Band-Aid. I didn't want to bring up the fact that it was the same day he'd left me.

His face dropped when he realized what I was getting at. "Please, let me buy your ring here."

"No. The ring you bought cost almost as much as my car. *My car.*" I shook my head. "It's too much."

He gently took my chin between his thumb and index finger to turn my face toward him. "After what I did, it will never be enough. I'll do whatever you want. I'm so sorry for putting you through that."

I shook my head at his apology. "What I *don't* want is for you to buy me a big fancy ring because you feel guilty. That's not how I am."

He pulled me into his arms. "Oh Zoey, no," he said in a low, soothing voice. "Please believe me when I say I know you don't care about stuff like that. Please don't ever think it."

He backed away and absentmindedly twisted a lock of my hair around his finger.

"Can I get a simple band instead?"

He shrugged his shoulders. "Will you at least look at the one I wanted to buy you? Then make up your mind?"

What the hell was I supposed to do? I was seriously wearing an engagement ring that cost almost as much as my Audi. Now he wanted to spend more money on the wedding ring, which would no doubt put the cost of jewelry on *one* little finger, well over the price of my car.

My fucking car . . .

"I'll look at it, Andy, but if I say it's too much, you need to listen to me. I don't want you trying to get your way once we get inside."

I pointed to my stomach. "Don't forget we're having a baby here. We shouldn't be spending so much money on material objects. She's going to need a lot of things you know . . . like diapers and food and—"

He leaned over and pressed his lips to mine, then pulled back. "Zoey, remember when you told me that the next time I had something important to say, to tell you to quit running your mouth?"

I smiled and nodded, because I very clearly remembered the conversation and realized he'd kissed me to shut me up.

"I'm telling you right now, don't worry about it." He grinned. "Everything will work out. We'll just talk about it later, okay?"

Seriously? How could I *not* worry about it?

We finally entered the store and spoke to the salesperson, who pulled out three wedding bands for me to look at. She set out a simple band, the diamond band that matched my engagement ring, and then the ring Andy wanted to buy me. She gave us a few minutes to look them over and talk.

The second she turned around, I pushed away the ring he wanted to buy me. Seeing the price tag was enough for me. I wasn't even going to try it on.

"It's beautiful, Andy, but it's way too much money."

He looked disappointed, but he didn't argue.

Starting with the traditional wedding band, I tried on the other two rings. With the plain band next to my engagement ring, I knew it wasn't the right ring either because my engagement ring was some serious bling, and the simple band was . . . well . . . too simple. *Crap.*

I slipped on the second ring and of course, it was perfect, and stunning. I tried to hide my smile, but that didn't happen.

"Well, look at that," he said quietly, smirking at me. "It looks beautiful, and it fits your finger perfectly."

Smartass. I looked at the price. "Oh look, it doesn't cost as much as an Audi. Even better."

Two can play at this game, Andy.

He chuckled. "Can I buy you *this* ring then, bossy?"

It really was gorgeous—a slim platinum band with diamonds all around it.

He nudged me in the side as a big, cheesy grin spread over his face. "Come on . . . just say yes."

Evil man.

I smiled because I knew I was going to let him buy it. I took off the ring and placed it back in the box.

It cost *several* thousand dollars less than the one he originally picked. He handed it to the salesperson and she set it aside and put the other rings back in the display case.

"Now it's your turn." I asked the salesperson to show us a wide, platinum band with a simple design around it. She pulled out that ring along with several others, and Andy began slipping the rings on his finger.

He chose the ring I liked.

"You know," I said, "just because it's the one I liked, doesn't mean it's the ring you have to get."

He smiled at me, his eyes lighting up. "But it's the one I want and the fact that you like it too . . ."

He handed the ring back to the salesperson along with his credit card.

"Can we go home now?" I asked as we stepped out onto the sidewalk. "I'm tired of spending your money."

The only things I had paid for since I arrived in New Zealand were the baby clothes and my wedding dress. I had a feeling if he had been with me when I found my dress, he would've paid for it too.

He pulled me in close to him and wrapped his arm around my shoulders.

"No. And it's our money now. All of it."

Once we were in the car, he looked over at me. "I'm hungry. What sounds good to eat?"

I thought about what I wanted for all of two seconds. "I want a burger and fries . . . with bacon."

I started laughing after he gave me a quizzical look.

"Did you just have your first craving?" A pleased smile took over his face.

"Actually, I think I did." I laughed, because he was exactly right. I hadn't had any strange, or normal cravings, for that matter.

He bent over the console of the car like he was going to kiss me, but instead he kissed my belly. "Good choice, baby girl."

We ate at a hole-in-the-wall burger place. After a delicious barbecue bacon cheeseburger and "chips" as Andy corrected me when I referred to them as fries, I was beyond stuffed. I would not be eating again until the next day. Oh the chips. Fuck American fries, they would never compare to New Zealand's chips.

After lunch, Andy insisted on doing a little more shopping, and we ended up going home with several bags full of All Blacks clothing for my nephews Jake and Alex and even some cute little outfits for our baby girl and my niece Mya. Later that evening, I made my man sit downstairs while I went upstairs to hang my dress in his closet so it wouldn't wrinkle.

I noticed there was room in his closet for some of my clothes so I dragged one of my suitcases onto the bed and began unpacking my clothes.

A while later there was a light knock on the door.

"Can I come in yet?" Andy asked through the door.

"It's your room, come on in."

He came through the door with a questioning look on his face when he saw what I was doing.

"I thought I'd unpack if it's alright with you."

He grinned, and went to his dresser where he pulled clothes out of drawers and crammed them into different drawers to make room for me. He transferred clothes from my suitcase into the drawers he'd emptied out.

As I turned to hang another dress in the closet, I heard him chuckle. When I looked back, his grin had turned suggestively mischievous. Swinging from his index finger was my new, red lacy underwear.

"How about that dance you promised me the other night?"

I could feel my face flush. Yes, I had told him I'd dance for him, hadn't I?

"You can't back out now, Beautiful," he teased.

"Fine," I said. "Get my iPod out of my purse and plug it in while I get ready for you."

I grabbed the fedora he bought in Cabo from the closet. He eyed it curiously as I gathered some lingerie from the drawer.

After I changed in the bathroom, I stuck my head around the door.

"You know, I'm a little fatter than the last time I did this, right?"

He shook his head and grinned. "You're pregnant with my child, Zoey. There is nothing sexier to me than that. Now, get your fine ass out here and dance for me, woman!"

"One lap dance coming right up, you Neanderthal!"

I noticed he'd retrieved a chair from the kitchen. My Andy, always prepared. Even if it was for a lap dance, he was ready.

When we were in Sacramento, I had come home a few times to find a chair in my bedroom with some sexy lingerie he'd bought for me draped over it. My man liked his lap dances, and I was always happy to oblige him. To say we were a very sexual couple would have been an understatement, and the very reason I was pregnant.

His favorite striptease had been when I danced to "Criminal" by Fiona Apple. That day, I had found some very racy black lingerie that barely covered any skin. I had no idea that dental floss came in black, but if he wanted me to wear it for him, I would. I held in a giggle at the comparison.

"Okay, Sexy. You know the drill. Strip . . . *completely,* and sit on the chair with your eyes closed."

He stripped, sat on the chair, and closed his eyes in record time. I slipped on the black heels from my suitcase, dropped his fedora on my head and fluffed up my wavy hair, then cued up the song I wanted on my iPod. As Joe Cocker's "You Can Leave Your Hat On" played, I stood in front of him.

"You can open your eyes now."

When he opened them, his jaw dropped as his eyes swept over my black lacy bra and thong, my flirty garter skirt, and thigh highs with delicate trim.

"You like?" He nodded and closed his mouth. "Good, and this time . . . you can touch me all you want."

And like so many times before, I danced for him. For the first time, I was dancing for him as my fiancé, and in his home country of New Zealand. He kissed and touched all over my body as I moved around him. By the time the song was over, my little dance was long forgotten, and I was straddling his lap as we devoured each other.

Not bothering to take my clothes off, he pulled my panties aside and I slowly sank down onto him. He stood, locked my legs around his hips, and carried me over to the bed, where he carefully laid me down and slowly, and gently, made love to me.

Later, he stripped off my clothes and we fell asleep, his arm wrapped around me, hand on my belly and his breath on my neck.

Chapter Thirteen

Zoey

A few nights before our wedding, I had a horrible dream. I had no idea what triggered it, but I was back in Sacramento on the day Andy left me, reading every single word he had written in the letter he'd left on my bed. Then I was running across the courtyard and finding his apartment empty. I was wondering why he'd left me when I hadn't done anything wrong. I woke up hurt and angry. Exactly like I had been that day back in August. It was only a dream, but it felt so real.

Andy slept peacefully beside me, which only triggered more turmoil inside of me. All the emotions were back, full force. I still hadn't talked to him about how much his leaving had hurt me. I wanted to get away from him for a while so I could calm down and I needed to be alone with Hannah. I decided to take my twenty minutes of "me time," go down to the beach, and cry it out. I glanced at the bedside clock only to find it was four thirty in the morning.

Slipping quietly from bed, I pulled on some clothes, found my iPod, and snuck downstairs.

At the door, I pulled on a hoody, grabbed a thick beach blanket and lantern, and headed to the beach. I didn't wander far from the house, and I left the back porch light on so I could find my way back easily. I found a spot on the cool sand at the end of the long path and sat, wrapping the blanket around me. I put the lantern aside and left it turned off, because light from the moon and the porch light clearly let me see my surroundings.

I scrolled to my playlist which I jokingly, yet appropriately titled "songs to cry to" and hit play. It had been a few days since I had taken my twenty minutes and I was ready for a good cry. The sweet crooning of Amos Lee singing the song "Colors" did not bring on the tears that it usually did. In fact, it made my anger worse.

The song talked about life, and all the colors metaphorically fading because the one you loved was gone. Everything but Hannah was gray. I felt the true meaning of the lyrics, because Andy had left me, but my twenty minutes was up, and I still hadn't cried.

I yanked out my earbuds and shoved my iPod into my pocket. I wasn't ready to go back inside, so I wrapped the enormous blanket tighter around myself and hoped the sound of the ocean would soothe me. I rested my hands on my baby girl, and stared off in to the blackness of the water.

The door slammed on the back of the house, startling the hell out of me. I turned to see Andy running across the deck with a flashlight in his hand. He was yelling my name, and he was in a panic.

I was too far away for him to hear me, so I stood and lifted the now lit lantern in the air to get his attention.

He ran down the path to me and skidded to a stop in the sand. "Zoey, what the hell are you doing down here in the middle of the night?" He moved in closer to me and tried to put his arms around me. I was angry and didn't want him to touch me, so I stepped back.

"You left me, Andy," I whispered and finally the tears came.

He moved closer, gripped the blanket, and pulled me toward him. I pushed him away as hard as I could.

He was shocked and hurt by my physical reaction. "Zoey, what did I do?"

"You fucking *left* me! How could you do that to me?"

The guilt in his eyes told me he knew exactly what I was talking about.

"Zoey, please . . . I was stupid, and mad, and scared."

"You broke my heart when you left, Andy. No, you *shattered* my heart in to pieces."

Gathering the blanket around me again, I lowered myself to the sand. He sat down next to me and put his arm around me. I was too distraught to push him away again.

I sat, sobbing, letting the wave of tears spill down my face and neck. After several minutes, I laid down, my back to him. I was still too upset to look at him. However, at least I was crying.

"I had to go see Dr. Jensen again. I couldn't stand sleeping at my apartment by myself. The only thing that kept me from falling apart was Hannah. She was my anchor, Andy. To you . . . and me."

He laid down behind me. "Zoey, I'm so sorry for what I did. What can I do to fix this? Can you ever truly forgive me?"

He wasn't getting it. I *had* forgiven him already, but I needed him to know how badly he had hurt me. I rolled over to face him and opened the blanket up so he could snuggle up to me.

A wave of relief washed over his face as he pulled me close and wiped the tears off my face.

He needed to understand what I was trying to say. "You don't need to do anything. It's been fixed, and you've been forgiven. I just relived that entire day in a dream, and I needed my twenty minutes, so I came out here."

"What do you mean twenty minutes?"

"Every day since I found out I was pregnant, I've given myself twenty minutes to sit and think, and to cry if I need to. I couldn't let myself get depressed again, Andy. I could *not* let myself slip back in to my old ways. I've worked too hard—"

He kissed my forehead. "Yes you have, Zoey. You amaze me every single day with your courage and strength. But I need you to tell me everything. I need to know how badly I hurt you so I can make it right," he said softly. "Even though you say it's fine now, it's obviously not."

We laid on the beach, and I told him about finding the letter. I told him how I couldn't even go inside his apartment because I knew he wouldn't be there. I told him about seeing all of his personal belongings gone. I told him about me pretty much going on autopilot to do what I needed so he could come back to me.

"Zoey, did you know you were pregnant before I left?"

"No, not for sure, but I suspected it. I was going to tell you the day you came home. I couldn't tell you over the phone when you were over two hours away from me. I wanted to talk to you face to face about it."

He pulled me closer and I felt his body shaking with emotion. "God, Zoey. I am so sorry for everything I put you through because I was being a selfish prick and only thinking about myself. I wish you would've told me, though. I never would've left if I had known."

Of course, I knew that. "I knew you needed time, but I didn't expect you to leave *me* because of what happened with Emma. Once you left, I realized what I needed to do. I had to let you go to New Zealand, my love, so I could try to find out what happened since Michelle refused to see you."

He let out a long, shaky breath. "Zoey, I don't deserve you. After everything I've done to hurt you. After what you've done for me to make my life right. I swear to you, I was coming home."

"You were?"

He nodded. "Yes. When you sent me the photo book for my birthday, it hurt to see what I'd left behind. I knew then, I'd never be able to live without you. I never told you, but when I read the note you left next to our picture, I made appointments with doctors and they ran every test under the sun to make sure there was nothing wrong with me. I'd just gotten the last of the test results two days before you arrived. Tamati took me to play rugby, and fishing one last time, because I was going back to Sacramento. You just beat me to the punch and got here first."

A shrill laugh erupted from my throat and I brought my face up to his for a kiss. "I'm sorry that you had to go through all of those tests for no reason, since I already had the answers you needed."

"I'd do every one of them again, Zoey. But, I'm honestly so happy that you came here and got to see New Zealand with me. And that you're marrying me here."

A grin spread across my face when I thought of all the things that had happened to get me back to him. "You're stuck with me now, Sexy. Your ring is on my finger, and your baby is in my belly. I'm everything you ever dreamed of, right?"

We laughed, and it felt good.

He scooted closer to me. "If I have to spend every day of the rest of my life showing you how sorry I am for what I did, I will do it, Zoey. You are my love . . . you are my life. Please, tell me I'm yours too."

I feathered kisses all over his beautiful face before planting one on his lips. "You are the reason I am here. Even if we couldn't have babies together, I would still want you. No matter what, *you* are my life."

I chuckled at what my next words were going to be. "And because of the flu, failed birth control, and an amazing time on the hood of your car, we now have Hannah. Life can't get any better."

His deep, rumbling laugh resonated the air between us. "It was also because of you and that short skirt of yours."

I pulled his face to mine for a deep kiss. "Do you think I can get a replay of that incredibly hot night? Right here on the beach? Well, minus the Camaro, of course."

I could feel the heat from his gaze on me as his hands slipped down to rid me of my jeans and panties.

"I think that can be arranged . . ." He kissed me one last time before his head dipped below the blanket and he slowly made his way down my body.

Chapter Fourteen

Zoey

The day of our wedding, I woke up from a very peaceful sleep and found an envelope with my name on Andy's pillow.

The last note I'd had from him told me he was leaving me. I knew this note wasn't the same as that last one, but my heart clutched in my chest just the same. I picked up the thick envelope and took a deep breath before I lifted the flap. Inside, I found a note and a rather large wad of money. *What the heck?*

I unfolded the paper and read his note.

Zoey - I am going to stick to the "it's bad luck to see the bride before the wedding rule" and meet you on the beach later. Iria is waiting downstairs for you and you'll both be going for a relaxing day at the spa. Massage, hair, makeup, nails, and anything else you want. Thank you for making me the happiest man on the planet today, and every day. Have a good time at the spa. I can't wait to see you later. I love you, Beautiful.

Andy

I folded up the letter and put it back in the envelope, then stashed the cash in my wallet. I had no clue how much money it was since it wasn't American currency, but the stack was thick and seemed like a crapload of money. I took a quick shower, threw on a dress and sweater with some ballet flats, and headed downstairs to meet Iria. She and Tamati had arrived home the night before.

I was so excited I practically skipped into the living room. "You ready to go get pampered, Iria?" I bounced on the balls of my feet in anticipation.

"Oh yes, Zoey, I am really looking forward to this." She was grinning from ear to ear. "A.J. is very generous." She held an envelope exactly like the one he'd left for me except with her name in Andy's easily identifiable handwriting.

"He sure likes spending his money these last few days," I commented.

"Well, he has enough of it," she said nonchalantly as she picked up her purse and keys. "Let's go get spoiled."

I wasn't quite sure what to make of her remark about his money. I mean, I knew he had some money from his parents' life insurance, but I hoped he wasn't going to start blowing it all on silly things.

He wasn't normally like that, but money did strange things to people sometimes. Even though he said everything he had, was now mine too, to me, it was still *his* money. He'd had it before me, I was doing fine on my own, and he would get his job back at the shop when we went home to Sacramento.

But that was a topic for another day, and a conversation I'd definitely have with him. At this moment, it was time to get ready for my wedding.

When we checked in at the spa, the attendant whisked us out onto a small private patio where a breakfast was set up for us. Of course, Andy would know I'd be hungry. Jeez, we were really being spoiled.

By the time we left the spa, we had both been fed, massaged, waxed, painted, and our hair and makeup done.

My hair was styled in a gorgeous waterfall braid with a loose side-bun, just behind my ear. Wavy tendrils fell around my face and to top it off, they fastened an enormous white and yellow flower—a Mount Cook Lily—at the back of the side-bun. It was a native New Zealand flower chosen by the hairdresser to complement my Maori jewelry. I knew Andy would love the fact that I was embracing New Zealand.

I asked the girls at the spa to take a few pictures of Iria and me while they were doing our hair and makeup. I sent them to my friends and family back home since they were missing my wedding day.

They pretty much freaked when I'd called them the week before to tell them about the wedding. They weren't upset about us getting married, but they were surprised we were doing it right away, and in New Zealand.

After I explained to them how excited we were to be getting married on the beach in front of Andy's home, they understood and were happy for us. They made me promise to let them throw us a party when we came home.

Iria and I arrived at the house to see Andy and Tamati down on the beach. Iria and I looked at each other curiously, wondering aloud what they were doing down there.

We dressed in Andy's bedroom while the guys dressed in Tamati and Iria's room. As Iria fastened the veil to my hair, I heard the marriage celebrant knock on the door. She was right on time.

We stood at the window and watched Andy, Tamati and the marriage celebrant walk down the path to the beach. From what I could see of Andy, he looked gorgeous.

I could not wait to meet him on that beach and become Mrs. Andrew James Tate.

"Zoey, it's time," Iria said. "You look absolutely breathtaking."

"You look stunning too, Iria. Your dress is gorgeous. Tamati is going to be thrilled when he sees you." She looked so pretty in a floor length dress similar to mine, but in a light peach color that looked amazing with her dark hair and skin. I smiled. "Thank you so much for everything. I wouldn't be here without you."

We walked out of the house and down the path toward the beach where Andy, Tamati, and the marriage celebrant were waiting for us.

My delicate, white dress and long veil were simple, yet ideal for a beach wedding. I went barefoot, as did everyone else, so I felt relaxed and free when I paused at the edge of the beach. Iria gave me a friendly hug and walked down to join the others.

Tamati and Andy were dressed similarly too—Andy in natural colored linen pants, and white long-sleeved shirt with the sleeves rolled up to his elbows. Tamati was dressed in khaki pants, and also wearing a long-sleeved white linen button up shirt.

I could not take my eyes off Andy. He was smiling like I'd never seen him smile before. He looked truly happy, with not a care in the world. I could honestly say I had never seen him like that. I smiled and made my way across the beach toward him.

Apparently, he couldn't wait any longer for me, because he met me halfway.

"What are you doing?" I whispered when he stopped in front of me.

"Your dad is supposed to be walking you down the aisle today. Will you let me do it?" he asked and offered me his hand.

A surprised smile spread across my face at his thoughtfulness, so I placed my hand in his and we walked the rest of the way together.

"Just Say Yes" played quietly in the background and I realized I'd been clueless at how he'd gone all out to make our day special.

"Zoey, you look beautiful," he said quietly. "You're glowing."

"Thank you. You are quite handsome yourself, Mr. Tate."

After I passed my flower bouquet to Iria, we faced each other hand in hand. The celebrant spoke about love and commitment to one another. She asked if we understood the ties that bound us together, the true meaning of unconditional love and forgiveness required of us both, and if we chose to love each other through good times and bad.

We both responded with a contented, "Yes."

Nope, no traditional "I do's" for us.

My eyes welled up with tears, as did his while we held each other's gaze.

"Zoey, please repeat after me," I heard the celebrant say from somewhere outside our bubble.

I listened to her and repeated: "I, Zoey Lynn James, take you, Andrew James Tate, to be my legal husband."

She smiled and nodded, letting me know to continue with my own personal vows I had written to him.

"Andy, I choose you to be my husband, my best friend, my lover, and the father of my children. I promise to trust and respect you, to laugh and cry with you. But above all, I promise to love you, with all that I am, unconditionally, forever."

When we had talked about writing our own vows, we had decided not to speak of death in them. There would be no "till death do us part" or anything like that. There had been too much death already.

We wanted to concentrate on life. Our beautiful life.

Andy smiled shyly and brushed a single tear off his cheek as the celebrant asked him to repeat after her.

His voice trembled when he spoke: "I, Andrew James Tate, take you, Zoey Lynn James, to be my legal wife."

I loved the happy, peaceful grin that eased over his face as the words left his lips.

The celebrant gave him a nod to continue with the vows he had written.

"My beautiful Zoey . . . today I take you to be my wife. I promise to trust you, respect you, and love you with all my heart. I will be a loving and kind husband to you, and father to our children. Today, I have everything I've ever wanted in my life, and to share it all with you, is a gift. Thank you for saying *yes*."

We both smiled at the last part, and with shaking hands, we exchanged rings.

The celebrant asked us to rejoin our hands.

"Zoey and Andrew, cherish each other, respect each other, and above all, *love* each other. I now pronounce you husband and wife. Andrew, you may kiss your bride."

He held my face in his big hands and kissed me gently on the lips. When our wedding kiss ended, we pressed our foreheads together, eyes closed, to savor the moment.

It was something we had done several times during our relationship. When either of us was having a bad day, or we needed to take a moment to gather our thoughts, it was our secret, silent way of leaning on each other for support or whatever else we happened to need at the time.

"I love you Zoey," he whispered.

"I love you too."

We kissed again, and then held each other on that sandy beach until someone finally cleared their throat and brought us back to reality.

Andy bent over and placed a kiss on my belly. "I love you too, Hannah."

It wasn't until then that I noticed a photographer taking photos. Andy turned up the volume on his iPod dock, and for the next hour, we posed for photos as all of the songs that held special meaning to us played.

He even threw in "Bad Romance"—the song I had been singing when we met. Andy asked me to dance on the beach with him when a song that I'd never heard came on. Andy said it was "In Her Eyes" by Joshua Radin. The melody was beautiful and the lyrics brought tears to my eyes as he sang the words to me while we danced. He couldn't have chosen a better wedding song to suit us.

Afterward, Iria and Tamati joined us for a few dances. I danced with Tamati and talked with him quite a bit since I hadn't met him yet. I quietly thanked him for watching out for Andy. He was a good man, loyal friend, and treated his wife like a queen.

Not to disappoint my family, I asked Iria to take a few pictures of Andy and me to text to our families and friends. With the photos finished, and a bit of dancing, the weather was getting chilly so we went inside the house.

Andy led me up the stairs and into his bedroom where he sat down on the edge of the bed, and pulled me onto his lap. Our arms wrapped around each other, we sat in silence and enjoyed the moment together.

"Thank you for today, Andy. It was perfect," I said quietly as he stared up at me.

"Stand up and let me look at you, Beautiful." When I stood, Andy took my hand and twirled me around. "Wow," he said. "You're gorgeous. The dress and veil, your hair, your flower and jewelry, my *wife* is exquisite."

I picked his left hand up and kissed his wedding ring. "*You* are gorgeous, husband." I couldn't help but smile. "I knew you were handsome before, but when I saw you down on the beach waiting for me." I paused. Of course, he was handsome, but today, he was so much more than that. "Andy, you looked so . . . serene. I've never seen you like that before."

He smiled and kissed my cheek. "It was because of you and Hannah, Zoey. When I saw you standing there in your wedding dress, with my child growing inside you . . ." He paused, shook his head, and his eyes filled with tears.

I took off my veil and returned to his lap. "Hey, I thought we were going to try and stop crying for a while?"

Andy wiped the tears from his eyes with the backs of his hands, and sat there looking completely vulnerable. "I can't help it," he admitted. "When I saw you, I knew this was where I was meant to be. Like you said, I was spared from dying in the accident for a reason. I knew the second I saw you on the beach, you were right. You and Hannah are the reason."

"Thank you for saying that, my love. We only get one life, and we need to live it to the fullest. No looking back."

We sat silently for a while longer before he spoke. "So, Mrs. Tate, would you like to go out to a nice dinner tonight to celebrate?"

"On one condition, we take Iria and Tamati too."

He smiled. "I already made the reservation for the four of us. Let's go."

"When did you have time to do all of this? A photographer, music at our wedding, dinner reservations, spa day for Iria and me. That's a lot of work."

He laughed heartily. "It's a secret . . . and you sleep . . . a lot."

I smiled and rolled my eyes at him.

Chapter Fifteen

Zoey

A few days later, I was pulled from a wonderful dream I was having about our wedding by Andy rubbing my bare belly with his big, warm hands. I opened my eyes and looked at his pillow, but he wasn't there. He had scooted down the bed, so his face was level with my stomach. He was kissing my belly and talking softly.

"Do you know how adorable it is that you are down there talking to our baby while I'm sleeping?" I propped myself up on my elbow.

He looked up at me and grinned contentedly. "I can't wait till she can talk back to me, Zoey."

I smirked. "You won't be saying that when she's a teenager. Especially if she takes after me, she'll be talking back all the time, and it won't be pretty. She's probably going to cuss constantly, just like I did."

I had been good lately with my language, though. I tried to be more aware of what I was saying because we did *not* need a two-year-old Hannah telling someone to fuck off.

Andy sat up and moved to lay down next to me with his head on my pillow. "We'll figure it out together." He smirked at me. "By the way, I love your filthy language. It's kinda hot."

I laughed and slipped out of bed.

After we showered together and had breakfast, we took a blanket and walked down to the beach. We settled on the blanket, me lying on my back staring up at the sky and Andy on his side, facing me. I noticed him reach out to touch my belly, but he pulled his hand back after giving me a shy smile.

"It's okay," I said, giving him the go-ahead, but also curious as to why he pulled back. "I don't mind. She's your baby too, you know?"

"I know. I just don't want to drive you crazy. Every time I see her there—where she's growing inside you . . ." He trailed off to gather his thoughts. "I just want to hold her in my arms Zoey. I can't believe this is really happening."

My man had rendered me speechless with his sweet words and all I wanted to do was kiss him. So I did.

He kissed me back slowly, his tongue sneaking in to meet mine. The sweet, innocent kiss on the beach could easily turn hot and steamy.

"Mmm, you keep that up and we're going back inside," I whispered when he eventually pulled away from me. I rolled onto my side to face him, and scooted right up next to him until I couldn't get any closer. I draped my arm over him and nestled down in the crook of his neck and shoulder.

"You alright?" he asked quietly.

"Yes. I just wanted to be closer to you."

We laid silently on the beach a while longer before he stirred and spoke. "Zoey, do you want to go on a honeymoon?"

"We're kind of on one already aren't we?" I nuzzled in to his neck more and tried to scoot even closer. "We're in New Zealand, not working, and lounging on the beach. That counts right?"

He chuckled. "I suppose so, but do you want to see more of En Zed? Maybe go to Oz?"

Even though I knew he meant Australia when he said Oz, I still laughed. "Oz? I seem to have left my ruby slippers back in Sacramento."

He shook his head and chuckled. "Very funny, smartass. Do you want to go to Oz or not?"

I thought about it for a few minutes. When I started to speak, Hannah decided to have some sort of a spaz attack where it felt like she was kicking and wrestling, which in turn, reminded me of Andy's love of rugby. I reached down and rubbed my belly, giggling. My decision had been made for me by someone on the inside. "No Oz," I said as I met Andy's curious eyes. "I think I want to stay here and see where my husband grew up, and for you to show me all there is to see of New Zealand. And maybe catch a few rugby games along the way."

"It would be my honor to show you." He picked me up and carried me back to the house, then stopped at the door and opened it wide. "Mrs. Tate, when we got married I forgot to do something very important."

I grinned up at his smiling face. "What did you forget to do, Mr. Tate?"

After a smoldering kiss that lit every nerve ending in my body on fire, he said, "I never carried you across the threshold into our house." With that, he stepped through the door, pushed it closed with his foot, and took me up to bed.

After a beautiful two-week journey to see the sites of the New Zealand islands, we were back in Auckland at my doctor's appointment, the first one for Andy. I was twenty-two weeks along and seemed to be getting bigger by the day.

When the doctor told us what I might be experiencing, he mentioned I could have an increased libido and I almost laughed out loud. Just one glance over at Andy told me he was happy about that information. Not that it would be any different; we couldn't keep our hands off each other as it was.

Eventually, I would find out how wrong I was. When I felt the urge, I had to have him right then. There was no waiting. It was time when I said it was, and he never complained once about it.

Finally it was time for my ultrasound—the part Andy was looking forward to the most since he had only seen sonogram pictures and DVD's. Pictures and DVD's that were already weeks old by the time I arrived in Auckland.

When the doctor pressed the wand to my stomach, the whooshing sound of Hannah's rapid heartbeat filled the room. An immediate grin lit my face when I glanced at Andy. He was smiling, and his blue eyes came to life at the sound. I took his hand, and together we turned to face the screen where Andy saw his daughter for the very first time on a live screen.

During the ultrasound, the doctor pointed out Hannah's head, her arms and legs, her little hands and feet. The doctor explained to us how our baby was currently developing and that she could hear us if we spoke to her. I told the doctor I was having some discomfort in my pelvic area. He assured me, and a very concerned Andy, the mild pain was completely normal, because my body was stretching to accommodate the size of Hannah as she grew.

Andy asked the doctor a hundred questions. He was curious about everything. I enjoyed every second. I loved seeing the excitement on his face and in his eyes.

He was thrilled when she moved and seemed to stretch her little arms over her head. "Zoey, look at that!" he said in complete amazement when she did it again.

I laughed. "Oh, I can *feel* it. Pretty soon you'll be able to feel it too."

That very night, he *did* feel it. Little Hannah woke me up at about two thirty in the morning. I swore she was in there playing rugby or something. I shook Andy. He didn't wake up, so I shook him a little harder.

"Baby, wake up." Excited for him to feel her move, I yanked off the blanket and smacked him on the bare ass cheek.

He jumped a bit. "What the—"

"Get up!" I gave his butt cheek a pinch.

He groaned as he lifted his head. "What's wrong?" he mumbled. "Are you sick?"

Laughing, I picked up his hand and placed it on my stomach where I'd felt the movement. Not thirty seconds later, she rolled over or something. I wasn't sure, but it felt both miraculous and scary at the same time.

Andy sat up quickly and reached over and turned on the lamp, but didn't move his hand from me.

"Did you feel that?"

"Yeah, Zoey. She's amazing." He grinned from ear to ear as he watched my stomach intently.

Now that the light was on, I propped myself up on my elbows, and we both watched my belly to see if we could actually *see* her move. She moved again, and he quickly removed his hand.

"Keep watching the same spot and see if she does it again," I whispered. Sure enough, my stomach shook slightly as she repositioned herself inside me. "Talk to your daughter, Daddy."

He smiled when I called him "Daddy," scooted down the bed, and kissed right where we'd last seen her move.

The excitement in his eyes should have been a joyful moment for me, finally seeing him so happy, but honestly, my heart was breaking.

He was so ecstatic about becoming a father, but he had missed it the first time. If he had known about Emma, and then had to watch her die, it would have killed him. How he was with our growing baby, and me, showed me he would have never been able to cope with the loss. Especially after watching her grow for nine months, be born, and then die.

I hated what Michelle did, but I honestly sympathized with why she didn't tell him. She had been *married* to him. She had to have known how it would affect him. At least I hoped she did.

She'd had to grow a child inside her knowing what the outcome would be. Thank God we did not have to deal with that. My miscarriage was hard enough to cope with, but to carry a child full-term, only to have her die would be unbearable.

"Zoey, did you see her move?"

No, I missed seeing it because I was thinking about Michelle and Emma.

"See if she'll do it again," I whispered to him, avoiding his question.

He kissed the spot again.

"Hannah?" He rubbed his palm over my stomach as if he were trying to get her attention. "It's Daddy, give your mum a little hello kick."

Sure enough, my stomach moved. It wasn't much of a movement, but there was definitely something going on in there. We watched a while longer, but nothing else happened.

"She must've decided to go back to sleep," I said quietly as if trying not to wake her up.

After Andy shut off the light, I held my gorgeous man tightly, running my fingers through his hair until he fell asleep. Finally, my eyes became heavy and I drifted off myself.

Andy

"Let me help you, Beautiful." I took Zoey's hands in mine and helped her lower herself to the blanket I'd laid out on the grass at the cemetery the next day.

"Such a gentleman," she teased with a grin as she unzipped her jacket to make a little more room for her ever-growing belly. I couldn't believe how much our baby had grown since Zoey arrived in Auckland.

We'd been coming here nearly every day to visit my family. Having Zoey here to talk to was a huge help in getting the closure I hadn't realized I needed until she pointed it out to me. I thought I was okay until the news of Emma surfaced, but that sent me into a tailspin I couldn't get out of no matter how hard I tried. At one time, I had been Zoey's reason to fight for the happiness she deserved, and now she was my reason . . . for everything.

"Andy, are you alright?" Zoey asked.

She brought me out of my memories. God, if she only knew how right my life was now that she was here and we knew what really happened with Emma.

I dropped down on the blanket behind her and slipped my arms beneath hers. My hands came to rest on the roundness of my child growing inside my wife. My wife . . . my child. I finally had my own little family.

"Andy?"

I still hadn't spoken after getting lost in my contented thoughts. "Sorry, love. I was just thinking about you and our little girl and how insanely happy you've made me." I nibbled the side of her neck just below her ear, causing her to let out a quiet hum of pleasure.

"Speaking of you and our little girl . . ." My eyes met the black granite where my parents and sister were laid to rest. "Mum, Dad, Hannah-banana, we have another announcement to make."

Zoey chuckled and squeezed my hands after I said my sister's nickname.

"My beautiful wife had a great idea . . . we've decided to name our daughter after you, Hannah."

Zoey pulled my arms tighter around her and nuzzled her head into the crook of my neck.

"Do you think she'd be happy with our decision, Andy?" she asked quietly, sounding unsure of her idea.

"Yes, she would be thrilled. She's probably up there twirling around and laughing right now." My throat tightened from the memories of my sister spinning round and round every time she wore one of her frilly dresses. She was such a girly girl. All pretty dresses, bows in her hair and fingernail polish in every color of the rainbow. God, I missed her. Zoey couldn't have honored her any better by choosing to name our baby girl after her.

"Good," she said. "How are you doing? Like, how are you really doing? Is coming here and going to the accident site helping you?"

After pressing a kiss to the side of her head, I said, "It's helped so much—more than I thought it would, truthfully. In fact, I think I'm done going out to the site, but I'd still like to come here until we go home."

"Anything you want, you got it," she said confidently.

With a quick peck to her lips, I hopped up and jogged back to the car to get the chilly bin that I'd packed our lunch in. When I returned, we spread out on the blanket, had lunch, and talked. I almost felt free of the past that shackled me to this place. I loved and missed my family, but they were gone and I couldn't get them back. I had Zoey, our families in California, and a perfect baby girl on the way.

Sleeping until dawn the next morning, I woke to the sun beginning to shine through the windows. I knew it was time to move on. I shook Zoey lightly until she woke.

"Zoey," I whispered as she rolled over to face me. "I'm ready to go home."

She smiled sleepily. "As long as you're sure."

"One hundred percent." I kissed her bare shoulder and let her go back to sleep, then rolled out of bed and started planning our future.

The day had arrived for me to finally tell her what I'd put off for far too long.

Chapter Sixteen

Zoey

By the time I dragged myself out of bed and the shower, Andy had already arranged our return to Sacramento and was in the kitchen cooking breakfast. Once we were finished, he pushed his plate away and looked at me hesitantly.

"Zoey, I need to talk to you about something." He held his hand out to me and led me into the living room.

All week, I'd had the feeling that there was something on his mind, which he couldn't come right out and say. He would open his mouth to speak and then he would stop, as if he didn't know how to tell me what he needed to say.

It appeared that whatever he'd wanted to tell me was ready to come out. I was a bit worried, but I sat down on the couch next to him. "Spill it. I know you've got something on your mind. So let's get it over with."

He opened his mouth then quickly closed it again after he let out a frustrated breath.

"Andy, you're freaking me out. What is it? Are you in some kind of trouble? Wanted by the law? What?"

He actually started laughing at me.

Okay, so maybe it wasn't *that* horrible.

"No, it's nothing bad. My lawyer is coming over to go over papers for the house and . . . other paperwork," he said nervously.

He has a lawyer? "You have a lawyer?"

He nodded once. "He was actually my parents' lawyer, and he handled all their finances and their estate after they died."

Finances and estate? I was utterly confused. "What does this have to do with me?"

He took a deep breath. "We're married now, and everything I own is now yours too. If anything should ever happen to me, it will all go to you and Hannah."

Right then, I didn't want to hear *anything* about him dying. I frowned. "I see."

He scooted closer to me on the couch. "Don't be angry with me, please."

I shrank back onto the pillow. "I'm not angry. I just don't want to think about you dying, that's all."

"I know, Beautiful," he said in a comforting tone. "I don't want to think about it either. Let's get this taken care of so it's out of the way and we won't have to think about it again."

There was a knock on the door. Andy answered it and brought in a short, round man whom he introduced as Maxwell Davies. As we shook hands, I noticed the surprise on his face when Andy introduced me as his wife.

"Mrs. Tate, it's a pleasure to meet you," he said.

"Please, call me Zoey."

His eyebrows rose when I spoke. "You're American?"

"Yes, I am." I wondered if that was going to be an issue.

He set his briefcase on the table as he sat down on the couch. He opened it and pulled out folders full of papers.

"Mr. Tate," he said, "I've brought all the paperwork you've requested. Do you have a copy of your pre-nuptial agreement for my files?"

What the hell?

Andy shook his head. "We don't have one, Mr. Davies. Everything I own, I want to go to Zoey and any children we have. There is nobody left for it to go to."

What was happening here? A pre-nup? For what? *What am I missing?*

"Andy, what's going on?"

He took a breath and looked me directly in the eyes. "I have some money." He shifted in his seat uncomfortably and ran a hand through his hair. "I inherited from my parents."

Things were slowly clicking, but I was still in shock. "Do you mean money other than the insurance money I already know about?"

"Yes, I do."

So this other money must be the reason his house was paid off. He already told me he never touched the insurance money, and he was living off the money he made from working. "Why didn't you tell me?" I asked, unsure if I wanted the answer.

"It didn't seem relevant at the time, I guess. But now it is. It's in a bank here in Auckland."

Why did I suddenly feel like an outsider?

The two men in front of me, one of them being my new *husband,* had all this information that maybe I should have been aware of prior to marrying him.

"So what do you need from me?" I asked. "I'm so confused, Andy . . ."

Unable to sit still any longer, I stood and paced slowly back and forth. "How much money are we talking about?"

Did I really want to know the answer?

I lived comfortably with what I earned at the store and the shop, and the additional income from renting the apartment next door. With Andy's paycheck from the shop, we would be totally fine financially.

I only wanted him. I didn't need anything else he had. Thoughts went through my head as I looked around his house. The place was a mini mansion on the beach, in a wealthy neighborhood of Auckland. On the freaking beach!

He never hesitated putting his credit card down to pay for something. Ever. My rings, our honeymoon. His trip to Cabo. He spent money on whatever he wanted and didn't even bat an eye. I was becoming overwhelmed by my thoughts.

"Zoey, please sit down," he said. "Try to stay calm, okay?"

He was right. I needed to stay calm for Hannah's sake, so I sat.

"Someone better tell me what's going on," I said breathlessly.

"My grandparents owned a winery, Zoey. A very old, well known winery here in En Zed. When they passed away, my dad and Hamish inherited it and all of their life savings. They didn't want to own a winery, so they sold it and split the money from the sale, and the inheritance."

He paused and watched me for a minute. "My mum and dad invested some, bought this house and sent Hannah and I to private schools. My dad and Hamish still ran the winery even after they sold it. Then my parents died . . . and you know the rest."

Living in Northern California, I was well aware there was big money in a successful winery business.

Mr. Davies watched our exchange curiously. "Mrs. Tate, you didn't know about the money prior to today, am I correct?"

I looked at him like he had two heads, was he not paying attention?

"That's correct," I replied, with more irritation in my tone than I intended. "The only money I knew about was the money from the insurance, and I only found out about it by accident."

I turned to face Andy. He looked guilty, but guilty of what?

"I have two questions, Andy. One, why didn't you tell me? And two, how much money?"

It didn't really matter to me how much money it was, but it was enough that he hadn't wanted to tell me about it beforehand. I'd love him if he were a beggar on the street, or a mechanic at my dad's shop who had to live from paycheck to paycheck. I fell in love with the simple mechanic at my dad's shop.

But I needed to know what I was dealing with. He winced as he scrubbed his fingers hard across his jaw and took a deep breath.

"It's about ten mill—"

Holy fucking hell! I couldn't even hang around for him to finish his sentence. I stood and jogged out the door, not stopping until I hit the sand.

Chapter Seventeen

Zoey

Ten *million* dollars! *Are you fucking kidding me?* How could he not tell me something so . . . *huge?*

Was he insane? I felt like I was in another world. Who was this guy? Why didn't he tell me?

His hand wrapped gently around my wrist. "Zoey, please come back inside and talk to me."

I was furious and *embarrassed* of all things. My mind ran through all the hints he'd dropped over the time I'd known him and I just hadn't cared enough to ask him about it. The embarrassment came from words I'd spoken directly to him about rich people being assholes, while the entire time, he had millions of dollars sitting in a New Zealand bank. Frustrated, I plopped down onto the sand as my mind continued to go into overload.

"You know I don't care about your money, right?" I looked over at him.

He eased down beside me. "I know," he said. "I was going to talk to you about it on the drive home from Sonoma, but we ran in to Corey and everything went to shit."

I linked my arm with his and leaned over to rest my head on his shoulder. "Why didn't you tell me before we were married?"

"Would it have made a difference, Zoey?"

"Yes, it would have."

He shoved his bare feet under the loose sand, picked up a handful of it, and began sifting it through his fingers. "Why would it matter?" he asked hesitantly. "Would you have still married me?"

I smirked. "Yes, I would've still married you, because I love you. It would be ridiculous to *not* marry you because you have too much money." I was finally able to look him in the eyes. "I would have agreed to a pre-nup."

He let out an irritated sigh. "It's not like I asked for the money. There was nobody else it could go to since I'm the only one left besides Hamish, and he already had his half. My inheritance has been sitting here in En Zed for years. I never tell anyone about it because I don't want people treating me differently or using me. The only reason I even transferred the insurance money to my account in the States was for emergencies, or if I wanted to buy a house or something. And then when you found out about it, and you didn't treat me differently . . ."

He paused, and then laughed at the memory. "You never even talked about it again, Zoey. I should have just told you about the rest of it then because I trusted you."

"I'm sorry, Andy. I know you didn't ask for it, and that's not what my issue is. I also know how it feels to have something, then have someone try to steal everything right out from under you."

He shook his head. "I know you wouldn't do that. I want to share the money with you, to use it to take care of you and Hannah in case something ever happens to me."

He absentmindedly brushed my hair over my shoulder as he spoke. "Even if you turn around and divorce me now, I'll still take care of you because you're the mother of my child, and because no matter what, I will always love both of you."

I raised my head off his shoulder and looked up at him. "I'm not going to divorce you, silly, but you still should've told me before we were married. You could have at least given me the choice to decide what I wanted to do about it."

"I'm sorry. I was just so happy about the baby and that you were here. It was bad judgment on my part and I'm sorry."

I wasn't sure what to do. I knew the money was inherited, but I was still upset he hadn't told me about it.

But he's telling you about it now, Zoey. Fuck.

"Did Michelle know about the money?"

Holy shit, I had no idea where that question even came from. It just came out of my big fat mouth.

He shook his head. "No. I didn't tell her because of the way her family treated me, right from the beginning. I wanted them to like me for who I was, not for what I had. If they knew, they would have tried to change me, and the way I am, or they would have changed their minds and approved of me because I had money. But none of that even matters anymore. I am married to *you,* not her."

"I want papers drawn up. I know you want to take care of us, but ten million dollars? Can you put it in a trust fund for Hannah instead? I don't want anything like that from you."

He shook his head again. "No. It's not what I want to do. We're married now, and I want to share everything I have, equally."

"What about what I want?" I withdrew from him. "You seem to be making choices for me about a few things here, Andy. You leave Sacramento without even talking to me and now you're trying to force me in to this." I stood and brushed the sand off my pants. "I need some time alone to think."

Turning back toward the house, I left him sitting alone on the sandy beach. As soon as I walked inside, I slipped my bare feet into a pair of shoes, threw his All Blacks hoody over my head, grabbed my purse, and headed out the door. I was halfway up the driveway when he caught up with me.

"Where are you going?"

"I don't know." I continued walking. "Away from here. Please leave me alone . . . just for a while."

All I wanted was time to think, by myself. Time to work things over in my head without his presence to influence me.

He gently grabbed my hand. "Please, Zoey. Don't go . . . please don't leave me . . ."

I stopped and turned to him. The alarm in his eyes was apparent.

"Let me go, Andy. I'm not leaving you. I just need some time to think. Please, just give me my twenty minutes."

Instantly, he released my hand.

I didn't miss the hurt and rejection in his eyes, but I turned around and started back up the driveway anyway because I needed to walk . . . and think. And calm the fuck down.

I had no idea where I was going, but after walking several blocks, I looked behind me and found that I was being followed. I knew it was Andy from the way he walked, but he was hanging back to give me space.

Continuing to walk, I pulled out my phone and sent him a text.

> *How am I supposed to be alone to think with you following me?*

I entered a small park and sat on one of the benches that faced the sidewalk. My phone pinged with a text from him.

> *I don't want you walking around by yourself. Just pretend I'm not here.*

He was right. It wasn't too smart of me to take off on my own like that in a country that was foreign to me. I sent him a very honest and heartfelt reply.

> *I can't pretend you're not there. I can feel you all around me, and part of you is growing inside me. You're everywhere that I am . . .*

Just the thought of Hannah brought tears to my eyes, so I closed them, and counted to five, letting myself calm down. He wanted to give us everything, and in his mind, I was refusing it. I wanted *him,* and if he came with money, I would get over it.

He entered the park a few minutes later and knelt in front of me. It was then that I noticed he hadn't put shoes on before he left the house.

"Please come home and we'll figure it out together. We can work this out."

I draped my arms over his shoulders and down his back, my forehead pressed to his.

"I'm sorry for walking away," I said softly and kissed his forehead. "You're barefoot. Why didn't you put on shoes?"

He looked at his feet as if he didn't realize he wasn't wearing shoes.

"I saw you through the window when you were leaving," he admitted. "I guess I just didn't think about it."

I made it several blocks from the house, and he followed me. *Barefoot.*

"Let's go back so we can figure this out," I said quietly.

He breathed a sigh of relief and whispered, "Thank you."

We stood and walked hand in hand back toward his house. Was I ever going to be able to call his home *ours?* I hoped I could. Halfway back, my cell began blaring "God Save the Queen" by the Sex Pistols.

Andy looked at me curiously. "It's Justin," I said laughing, so he knew who was calling, and why the ringtone was so fitting.

"Ahh, I see."

"Yes, my queen?" I joked in my worst British accent. "How may I be of assistance this wonderful evening?"

Justin squealed on the other end of the line. "Zoey? Guess what?"

He was so loud I had to pull the phone away from my ear. "Um, what's got you so excited, Justin?"

I heard Will in the background telling Justin to calm down and tell me something already.

"We bought a house!" he squealed again.

"Oh that's great," I replied. "Put me on speaker so I can talk to Will too."

I put my phone on speaker as well.

"Zoey!" Will shouted.

"Hey, Will," I said, happy to hear my friend's voice. "Andy is here with me. Tell him your good news."

"Hey guys," Andy said. "What's up?"

In unison, they both yelled, "We bought a house!"

Andy grinned. "Ah, sweet as. Congratulations."

Will and Justin laughed.

"I have no idea what that meant," Justin said. "But thanks, you big hunk of man, you."

The guys and I laughed as Andy turned a nice shade of red. They loved to tease him about how handsome and sexy they thought he was. He was very fond of them too after they had taken him to the hospital after my accident.

After they begged Andy to explain to them what "sweet as" meant, he told them that it was the Kiwi version of *cool* or *awesome*.

They told us they'd be moving out of the apartment in thirty days when escrow closed on their new place. After we congratulated them again, we hung up and strolled back to the house. Thankfully, Mr. Davies was gone because I could tell that Andy was going to be adamant about talking.

"Can we sit and talk about this, Zoey?"

Here we go.

I was ready to talk, but thought the conversation would go better and be over sooner if I had a distraction for just a bit longer. There was so much to think about, and required time for me to come to terms with the news I'd been given. "Let me make some hot tea first. Are you hungry? I can make something to eat too."

In the kitchen, we made sandwiches for lunch. While I sliced up the veggies, I thought about the big fat elephant in the room.

Ten million dollars.

What exactly was my issue, other than *not* being told about it? I couldn't think of any. We were married, so truthfully, everything that I had was his too. He had more than enough of his own money to last ten lifetimes. The most reasonable choice was to meet somewhere in the middle.

Fuck . . . I have so many questions. Time to get this straightened out, Zoey.

He wanted to share all his money, but he needed to know what *my* terms were going to be.

"Andy, I still want to work. I love what I do, and I love being a part of my family's business."

"I'd never ask you to quit your job, Zoey. If you want to work, I'm fine with that. In fact, it's what my parents did, and what I want us to do too. That's the way they raised us. They worked because they wanted to. All their paychecks went to daily expenses. Food, gas, household bills—basic things like that. The inheritance was to be used for the family. They only used it for big purchases, like this place, their cars, and our schooling. They took advantage of what it could do to enhance our lives, but they did it in a way where we still learned how to be responsible."

I understood what he was saying, and it made sense. Why would you have all that money and just let it sit there? It would be pointless not to spend some of it, but it would be stupid to waste it on things you didn't need.

"So, what do you want to do with the house here and the money?" I asked frankly as we sat down for lunch.

I needed to know what his expectations were, and he needed to know mine. We needed to make the final decisions together. I wasn't just going to do whatever he wanted.

Marriage was a partnership, after all.

He wiped his mouth with his napkin. "If you will agree, I'd like to pay off your car and the store. Especially now, since Will and Justin will be moving out, you won't have the income anymore from their rent."

Honestly, I hadn't thought about that since we'd just received the news that they were moving out. Their rent helped pay my bills.

"Do you want to pay off the store to be my business partner or pay it off for me?" I asked as he took a giant bite of his sandwich.

As he chewed, I thought about what I'd asked him. I didn't want him to pay off the store if he wasn't going to run the business with me. It didn't seem right for him to pay it off, then not be involved.

"Wait, don't answer yet." He needed to hear what I wanted to do.

"If you pay it off, I want you to be on the deed, *and* I want you to be my business partner. If you don't want to be involved in the daily business of the store, that is your choice, but I want it to be a fifty-fifty partnership."

He nodded. "Fine, I can live with that. What about buying a house for us?"

That was going to be harder for me to accept.

"Andy, I *love* where I live," I admitted. "Don't laugh, but I like the fact that it's on the second floor. To me it feels safer. More secure. I know with you moving in and Hannah coming in a few months, we'll outgrow it eventually. But for now, can we please stay there?"

"I love that place too, Zoey. We have lots of good memories there."

I started to say something when he covered my hand with his.

"I have an idea," he said as his eyes sparkled with excitement. "What if we move into the apartment above the shop, and get your place renovated. With the guys moving out, we'll have the whole floor above the store to live in."

Seriously? I loved the idea.

"I do believe I married a genius," I joked as a happy smile broke out over my face.

"Damn straight you did, Beautiful."

"Oh and he's a little cocky too."

He grabbed my hand, and put it on his crotch. "A *little* cocky, Zoey? Are you sure about that?"

He was hard and I gave him a little squeeze. "No, Sexy. Definitely *not* little. However, he is a little pervy."

We laughed as I pulled my hand away. "Back to business, Andy, pleasure later."

Chapter Eighteen

Zoey

My wheels started turning about designing and decorating new rooms. I loved the fifteen-foot tall ceilings, the exposed antique brick walls, and the lofty feeling of the apartments. If we combined them, we would have well over four thousand square feet to live in. It would be plenty of room for us, and plenty of room to grow.

So there I was, agreeing with his proposition.

"Yes," I said excitedly. "I love that idea." And I loved the smile that came over his face when I said *yes*.

We were talking, and we were making decisions together. That was good. It was *right*.

"Andy." I had an idea too. "Will you let me make you an En Zed room?"

He raised his eyebrows curiously and I laughed at his expression.

"I want to do a room, maybe a family room or something, I don't know yet . . . but I want the room to remind you of here. Remind *us* of here," I corrected.

He smiled. "What did you have in mind?"

Boy, my wheels were really turning now.

"I want to hang yours and your dad's surfboards, maybe get some All Blacks décor to hang up too. I want to make the room feel like it's actually *in* New Zealand. Maybe have some Maori and New Zealand artwork too."

"I like where you're headed with this."

I clapped my hands together with excitement. "Oh, and we'll get a big screen TV to hang on the wall so we can watch rugby."

He must have liked that idea, because he high-fived me.

"I love you, Beautiful."

For the next couple of hours, we planned our future. *Together.* It was wonderful. We talked about coming back to New Zealand every year for vacation. We wanted our children to know this place.

They would be half Kiwi, after all, as Andy pointed out with a massive grin on his face. He didn't find it amusing when I told him I wished I knew what the other half of them was, since I had no clue what I was.

"You're my girl, Zoey," he said. "You are beautiful, inside and out, and it's all that matters."

My insides did a little flutter from his compliment. I loved my man more than life itself.

We sat for so long I was getting uncomfortable sitting on the hard chair. "I'm going to clean up the kitchen, why don't you go find something to watch on TV."

He took our plates to the kitchen as Tamati and Iria arrived home from work within minutes of each other. I fixed them dinner while Andy sat with them, and told them we were leaving in a week to go back to Sacramento. We visited with them while they ate and told them about all our plans for when we got home.

We even made plans for them to come and visit us the following summer after we moved back into the newly renamed "loft" and after Hannah was born.

After their dinner, I excused myself to take a relaxing bath. It had been a long, draining day. I fixed another cup of hot tea to take with me, and said goodnight to everyone, then headed upstairs.

I slid down into the water and sipped my tea while the tub filled. I would miss this tub when we went back to Sacramento. It was huge. Big enough to comfortably seat two people. I thought about getting one like it for the renovation.

Making a mental note to talk to Andy about it, I finished my tea, washed, and conditioned my hair. I squeezed a large dollop of body soap onto the sponge and rubbed it between my hands to get it nice and sudsy.

"May I join you?" Andy asked from the doorway.

"Absolutely." I loved taking baths with him. They always reminded me of our very first meeting.

He had recently admitted to me that he liked the way I looked bent over cleaning his bathtub singing "Bad Romance." And, how much he liked the way my red lacy underwear had been showing above the waistband of my too baggy jeans. At least I knew why he liked the red panties so much.

He emptied his pockets, then shed his clothes and dropped them into the laundry hamper.

I scooted forward to let him sit behind me in the tub.

"Why is the water so cool?" he asked me once he was seated.

"I'm not supposed to take baths that are too hot because of the baby."

"I see." He took the sponge from my hand and gently washed my back.

"Can we get a bathtub like this one for our place?"

"You can get anything you like, Zoey. You don't need to ask."

I reclined against him after he rinsed me off.

"Okay, but I want you to like everything. You know it's going to take me a while to get used to this whole money thing."

He kissed my shoulder and slowly washed my front. He washed my entire body as we soaked in the tub, then I washed his. I paid extra attention to his feet since he had walked God knows how far with no shoes on because I was being a shit.

He was crazy-ticklish, so of course, I tortured him the entire time I scrubbed his feet. We ended up with more water on the tile floor than in the tub.

When we finished our bath, he dried me off starting with my shoulders, and worked his way down my body. He knelt when he reached my belly.

"You look beautiful pregnant, Zoey," he whispered as he smiled up at me.

He finished drying me and kissed my stomach before he stood. I took the towel and dried him off the same way he had done for me.

Afterward, I sat on the edge of the tub and pulled him closer.

"What are you doing, Zoey?"

He knew what I was about to do, but always felt it necessary to tease me about it. I smiled up at him and raked my nails lightly up and down the outside of his muscular thighs.

Andy groaned when I leaned forward and pressed a kiss to the head of his hardening cock. Without using my hands, I took him inside my mouth as he wound his fingers through my wet hair.

While slowly drawing him in and out of my mouth, I trailed my fingertips lightly up the backs of his thighs, over his ass, then up his back. I pulled him in deeper, as I dragged my nails down his back.

"Oh . . . fuck. That feels so good," he said between breaths.

I pulled my head back so just the tip of him was in my mouth and began pumping him with one hand as I swirled my tongue around him.

"Ahh, Zoey . . ." he moaned as I stroked him.

I looked up at him and his eyes flashed open and met mine. His eyes were completely glazed over in ecstasy and it turned me on to see him like that. Knowing it was me who was making him feel so good.

He loosened his fingers on one hand from my hair and began teasing my nipple. Oh fuck was right. With one simple touch from him, my body was on fire.

The harder I worked him, and the more he teased my nipple, the more I ached between my legs. Jolts of pleasure traveled downward from my nipple, so I pressed my legs together, intensifying the ache.

Holy mother of fuck, I was going to come, solely from him touching my nipples.

I stopped pumping him, took him all the way inside my mouth, and then released him completely. He groaned in frustration. I wrapped my hand around his base and began drawing him in and out of my mouth, sucking harder.

He ran the flat of his palm over my breast, lightly pinching my nipple between his fingers.

I pulled him from my mouth. "Mmm that feels so good."

Taking him back in, I moaned, moving my hand on him harder and faster. He started teasing my other nipple with his other hand. I slipped my free hand around him and dragged my nails down his back while he tugged, massaged, and squeezed my breasts.

My body began to throb and tremble. I squeezed my legs together tighter which intensified my orgasm. I whimpered from the pleasure coursing through me, and sucked him further into my mouth. Andy groaned as his orgasm ripped through him. His body jerked slightly, and he came as my orgasm subsided.

Holy fucking shit. I gently released him from my mouth and swallowed. He took my hands and helped me stand, but I wobbled a bit. He steadied me.

"Did you just come while you were doing that?" he asked huskily, his voice deep and sexy.

I nodded as I felt the heat rise in to my chest and face.

"That was fucking intense, Zoey," he whispered.

Yes, yes it fucking was.

He led me to the bed, where he pulled all the blankets back and tossed the pillows to the floor.

"Get on your knees facing the headboard," he growled.

Oh my. I did as he said because I was anxious to see what he had planned for me. Whatever it was, I knew I'd love it.

He knelt behind me. Trailing his hand down to the inside of my thigh, he urged me to spread my knees further apart. "Wider," he whispered, as he kissed my neck and back. He slipped his hands between my legs from behind, and slid his fingers inside me. He slowly moved them in and out.

I reached behind me, took his cock in my hand, and stroked him. He was already getting hard again.

It was going to be a good night. I turned slightly to kiss him. His fingers still moving inside me, his other hand came around to cup my breast and he teased my nipple again.

Oh my, he was good at that. I don't know if it was a combination of his hands being rough from work, because he was always so warm or just him in general. But, I was on the verge of orgasm again when he pulled his fingers away and backed up.

"Where are you going?" I demanded anxiously, because I was definitely not finished.

The next thing I knew, he was lying on his back and burying his face between my legs.

Yes, I was almost sitting on his face. Holy fucking hell, I was *not* expecting that.

I had never been in that position before, and just the thought of it made me burst in to a fit of giggles. I laughed for all of two seconds until his lips met my body and I gasped.

It felt so fucking good, but I was still a little embarrassed at the position. I didn't know why, it's not like he hadn't done it to me before, just not in that position.

I chuckled again at the thought, and he stopped.

"You know, this is supposed to make you come, not laugh," he joked.

I laughed again. "I just feel so . . . *exposed.*"

After a few moments, I had the nerve to look down at him. I could barely see his head past my belly, which sent me in to another fit of laughter.

"Zoey? Shut up and enjoy the ride," he commanded.

He licked, and sucked and groaned against me, sending the most mind-shattering vibrations directly to my clit. He slipped two fingers back inside me and began massaging my g-spot.

"Oh, Andy." I moaned as I began rocking my hips slowly against him.

He picked up the pace, and with his free hand, he gently raked his short nails down my back. I finally realized why it sent him over the edge. It felt like every nerve in my body was alight with desire.

I rocked my hips faster to match his pace as he dragged his hand down my back again. He gripped my ass in his big hand, and my body began squeezing tight around his fingers.

"Oh fuck, oh fuck . . . Ohh . . . fuck," I mumbled as my orgasm rendered me completely incapable of saying anything else.

He continued to stroke me inside, but I was completely over sensitized. "Oh fuck, you've got to stop," I whispered as the spasms continued.

My body went limp, and I had to grab the headboard so I didn't sit on the poor guy and smother him.

Once my orgasm subsided, he slid out from under me. I had never come so hard in my life. Shaking, I closed my legs and collapsed onto the bed.

"Jesus fucking hell, Andy," I muttered as I closed my eyes and threw my arm over my face.

He laughed as he walked his fingertips up my side.

I tried to smack his hand away, and he laughed harder.

"Did you enjoy that?"

He knew the answer, but was trying to get a rise out of me. I moved my arm and met his gaze, feeling my face flush. He rolled me onto my back, slid on top of me, and pushed himself inside me. He thrust slow and hard.

Fuck me. He's trying to orgasm me to death.

I was enjoying every fucking second of it.

Several minutes later, I was coming again and so was he. After we were both completely spent, he rolled to his side breathing heavily.

"Fuck Zoey . . . I think I need another shower."

I knew I did. I was soaked and sweaty.

I sat up and twisted my wet, uncombed hair in a messy knot. We stepped inside the shower and washed each other off. We barely had enough energy to brush our teeth, before we fell back into bed and passed out from exhaustion.

Chapter Nineteen

Zoey

One week later, we were on a plane back to Sacramento. Unbeknownst to me, Andy bought us Skycouch seating for our return home since it was an overnight flight. That meant we had an entire three-seat row all to ourselves. The underside of the seats popped up, so we were actually able to lay down side by side.

It was a bit cramped for me as big as he was, but I was in heaven because I could lie down and sleep.

We also may, or may not, have joined the mile-high club on our flight home. I would surely never tell.

My flight to New Zealand hadn't been too bad, but now that I was further in to my pregnancy and with changing planes twice, I was completely exhausted when we landed in Sacramento. Although, the layovers were at least long enough so we could get off the plane and walk around the airport.

As soon as we walked into our apartment, I went straight to the bedroom, crawled into bed, and fell asleep. It would be a mistake to go to sleep so early, but baby Hannah was running my life. I had no choice but to obey her. If my baby girl wanted or needed something from me, she got it.

My body was completely at her mercy.

Andy woke me up a few hours later. I showered, changed, and almost felt human again. *Almost . . .*

I was anxious to see my family, so I went across the courtyard to the shop. I snuck through the back door to surprise them, but apparently, nobody was surprised we were home. While I'd slept, Andy had gone over to apologize profusely for going off to New Zealand, at least to my dad and my brothers. My mom was out of the office running errands.

I received lots of belly rubs from my brothers and my dad while we visited in the empty customer lounge. I didn't even get any snide comments from Adam about my weight gain. He must have learned his lesson. That, or my loving husband had a chat with him about giving me shit all the time.

I'd only been at the shop visiting for a little while when my mom came barreling through the door.

"Mija," she called as I scrambled from the couch to hug her.

"Mom," I cried. "I missed you so much."

After she hugged me, she took my hands and held my arms out to the side to take in the view of my expanding waistline.

"You've grown so much since I saw you last. You look positively radiant."

She noticed Andy standing off to the side by himself.

"Oh, Andy honey," she said with tears in her eyes. "Welcome home, *mijo*."

I saw him blink back tears. He'd asked me months ago why my mom always called me *"mija"* and I explained to him what *mija* and *mijo* meant.

My mom was calling him "my son."

I knew he'd been nervous coming back to Sacramento after everything that happened, but my family was wonderful and caring so he was forgiven and welcomed back into the family.

"So, have you two decided on a name for my granddaughter?" she asked him, her arms still wrapped around his waist.

"Yes," he said. "We're calling her Hannah, after my sister."

My mom grinned and squeezed him again. "What a perfect name, Andy."

After we said our goodbyes to my family, we walked back across the courtyard to the apartment. Will was unlocking his door when we entered the lobby.

"Will?" I called as we climbed up the stairs to greet him.

A flash of orange fur came bounding down the steps after he opened his door.

Andy scooped up James. "Hey, you little shit." He scratched behind our cat's ears. "Have you been a good boy?"

Will shook his head as he stared at James. "He's been good, *most* of the time."

We laughed. Yep, that sounded like James.

"Wow Z," Will said when he got a good look at me. "You look like you swallowed a basketball, but you look amazing."

He invited us in, and we sat with him on the couch to catch up. Moving boxes were scattered all around the apartment.

"I'm gonna miss you guys living next door," I said sadly. "I'm so happy for you two, though." We talked about their new house until Justin came home from work.

To say he was happy to see us would have been a gross understatement. As soon as he walked through the door and saw us sitting on the couch, he started jumping around and getting all hysterical.

I think he even clapped a couple times he was so happy to see us.

"Dude," I said. "Chill out before you crap yourself."

Everyone erupted with laughter. Justin had tears in his eyes from laughing so hard by the time he caught his breath.

After family dinner at my parents' house that night, we stayed long after my brothers and their families left. We sat down with my mom and dad to tell them about the inheritance, and our plans for the store and apartments. They were taken aback with the news, just as I had been. They asked tons of questions, but once we explained the way Andy's family had lived, and how we planned to do the same, they were one hundred percent behind us.

My dad was also thrilled Andy was going to be involved in the store. He was ready to retire, but worried about me taking on all the responsibilities by myself. He didn't have to worry any longer and gave us the go-ahead to remove him from the deed. I felt a little sad to do that, because it had been my dad and me from the beginning. But, being my dad, he insisted and then said how proud he was of me for getting the business as far as I did, with barely any help from him.

With my parents' blessing in regards to the store, Andy and I were moving forward with our lives. As a team. It felt amazing and scary all at the same time, but I knew we would succeed because we'd never give up on each other or our life together.

Thanksgiving Day had arrived, and we had invited Hamish and Sarah to join my family at my parents' house. They volunteered to drive Andy's truck and trailer back from Sonoma so we wouldn't have one more thing to deal with. Everyone was being so helpful and supportive. It was fantastic.

When Hamish and Sarah arrived, Sarah parked their car while Hamish drove the truck and trailer over to the shop.

She exited the car and gave me a big hug. "Zoey, I've missed you both so much. You look gorgeous."

When she released me, Hannah began kicking like crazy and I rubbed circles on my belly as I stood talking to her. Sarah watched me with a hint of sadness in her eyes as I tried to soothe my baby. She had told me once before she'd never been able to conceive, but always wanted children.

"Do you want to feel her kick, Sarah?"

She nodded happily and put her hand on my stomach. I rested my hand on hers, and the next time Hannah kicked, I moved our hands to the spot. We moved our hands all around my stomach, feeling Hannah kick and move until the guys came back from the shop. They rounded the corner and stopped dead in their tracks when they found us standing there laughing.

With all four hands on my belly, it must have looked a bit odd.

The expression on Andy's face was of pure love and adoration. The expression on Hamish's face was of love and sadness. I didn't want him to be sad, so I held my hand out to him.

"Hamish, come and feel her kick."

He jogged over smiling and placed his hand in mine. I set it where Hannah was kicking. Andy came and stood next to me, waiting for his turn.

It was his favorite thing to do.

A day never went by that he didn't have his hands on my belly, or wasn't talking to Hannah and kissing my stomach. In fact, that was how he would lull us both back to sleep when she woke me up in the middle of the night. On rare occasion, he even sang what he told me was an old, Maori lullaby his mother had sang to him as a child.

It was perfect, and I could not wait until she was born so Andy could hold her in his arms. I knew it sounded unusual to be excited for him to hold her, instead of me, but she was growing inside me. I had been holding her since the moment she was conceived.

Without a doubt, I wanted to hold her in my arms too, but the love I had for Andy, and the love he held for Hannah and I, made me want to give him the world.

We were his world, and all that mattered to him. He made sure to tell me so daily.

After the baby visiting, the guys took Hamish and Sarah's luggage upstairs to the guest bedroom. They were staying with us for a few days, so we had bought a new bedroom set for the guest room.

"Wow, this is a great space," Sarah said as she examined our apartment from bottom to top. She looped her arm through mine and smiled. "Show me where you're going to put the nursery for my great-niece."

"Right this way," I said. As we walked toward the hallway, I pointed at the wall that separated the two apartments. "This wall is getting knocked down to start with, so Hannah's bedroom will actually be the current guest room." Quickly, I showed her the guest room where she and Hamish were going to sleep then led her next door to the other apartment Justin and Will had vacated.

"Over here, we're going to add on to the kitchen and dining room, add three more bedrooms, a full bath and a half bath," I explained as we wandered around each room.

Sarah gave me a sly grin. "That's a lot of extra bedrooms, Zoey."

Laughing, I placed my palms on my growing belly. "Well, your nephew has already decided he wants a big family, so I'm preparing myself for three or four. I have four brothers, so I think that's about all I can handle."

"That's wonderful, Zoey." Sarah hugged me. "Thank you so much for giving A.J. everything he's always wanted . . . and so much more."

"He's my everything, Sarah. I would give him my life."

"You already have Zoey," she said quietly as we rounded the corner of the building.

When we found the men outside in the courtyard, they were in mid-conversation.

"I do have one more question," Hamish said to Andy. "What about an outside play area for Hannah? With grass to run around in."

Andy saw us when we came into the courtyard and immediately smiled. "What do you think about doing something with the courtyard Zoey?"

"Well, I thought about adding an extra section of fence to the other end so we'll have a completely fenced in lawn area," I explained. "The kids can play out there safely and we can have barbecues and things like that."

Andy agreed. "That sounds good, and there's enough room to play rugby."

We all laughed at him.

"One track mind when it comes to rugby," I joked.

Hamish and Sarah nodded in agreement.

When we arrived at my parents,' Andy, Hamish and Sarah carried the food in while I brought the gift bag containing souvenirs from New Zealand for our nephews and niece. Once inside, Jake and Alex came screaming into the kitchen when they found out Andy was home. He knelt down on the floor to greet them, and they slammed against him, knocking him over onto his butt.

"Hey guys!" Andy said, over-exaggerating his accent for them. "How are my favorite nephews doing?"

He looked back and forth between them like he was watching a tennis match, as they both talked at the same time.

"I want Aunt Zoey's chocolate pie," Jake said, while little Alex chanted, "Pie, pie, pie!"

I was smart this year and made two. Turns out baby Hannah liked chocolate cream pie too, because I'd had to eat a slice of it with my breakfast.

Andy stood and held his hands out to Jake and Alex. "Hey, come with me, we brought you pressies from En Zed." The boys each grabbed a hand, and he led them away.

When the three of them came back into the kitchen, the boys were dressed from head to toe in All Blacks gear. They were wearing All Blacks hats, scarves, pullover hoodies, and black Adidas track pants with stripes down the legs. They were each carrying a rugby ball too.

Andy had even put his hoody on to match them. *Yep, I need a picture of this.*

I pulled out my cell and situated them on the couch, Andy in the middle, and a nephew on each knee. The three of them had big toothy grins on their faces when I snapped the picture.

A-freaking-dorable. "This picture is definitely going in a frame on the wall." I showed the picture to them.

For Thanksgiving dinner, we decided to go completely traditional, and make turkey and all the fixings. We would always sneak some tamales or some other Mexican dish in, but this year Noah and Jess wouldn't be here, and neither would Adam and Angie. Jeremy was here alone, as usual, but he and Andy got along well, so they played poker and talked about cars.

Mya started crying from the other room a while later. She had been asleep since before our arrival. Heather started to get up, but Andy beat her to it.

"Can I get her, Heather?" he asked eagerly.

Heather smiled up at him as she sat back against the couch to relax. "She's all yours, Andy. Go get some practice for when your little girl arrives."

After Andy left the room to get Mya, I looked over to Heather. "Don't be shocked if she comes out wearing All Blacks footy pajamas." I knew he'd bought her some, and sure enough, Andy came out carrying a happy Mya in her All Blacks outfit. Everyone said how adorable she looked, so I took a picture of Andy and Mya together for our album.

Mya giggled and attempted to kiss Andy on the cheek, but she ended up licking him instead. When her tongue touched the stubble on his face, her little mouth puckered up like she had tasted a lemon.

Yep, I took a picture of that too. It was so cute.

He sat holding Mya on his lap until she got fussy and needed to be fed. He handed her off to Heather and then patted his lap, so I took Mya's place on it. I sat carefully, so I didn't squish him. I hadn't gained that much weight, but my belly was sticking out quite a ways.

Thankfully, I was all belly so far. I'd finally gone up a bra size too, although I didn't mind that part. I would eventually, when they were too big, but for now I was happy with an actual C-cup without padding.

"Hey," he whispered into my ear as I rested my head in the crook of his neck. "Have I told you lately how beautiful you are?"

Yes, my heart just melted in to a puddle of mush. I hugged his neck with one arm and kissed his cheek.

"You tell me every day, but I'm glad you decided to tell me again right now," I said quietly. "I'm feeling a little . . . *round.*"

Andy wrapped one arm around my back, resting his big hand on my hip and rested his other hand on our daughter. He took a deep breath and let it out. "I can't believe it's been a year."

Unsure of what he meant, I asked. "A year for what?"

He smiled. "Since I took the job at your dad's shop. We've known each other a year."

I couldn't help but laugh at the way everything had turned out for us.

"And look where we are now," I joked pointing to my belly. "Married with a baby on the way. Who would've thought?"

Definitely not me, that's for sure.

He squeezed me a bit tighter. "I'm so happy, Zoey."

I squeezed him back, nestled in a little closer, and closed my eyes. "Me too, baby . . . me too. I love you so much." I sat snuggled up on my man's lap, wrapped in his warm arms, in complete bliss.

The next thing I knew, he was waking me up, and I was on the bed in my old bedroom. He must have picked me up and carried me in here after I fell asleep on his lap in the living room. He was always very gentle when he needed to wake me up, which was getting to be more frequently as tired as I was all the time. I would wake to him rubbing my back, or running his fingers through my hair.

Lately though, when Andy woke me up, I'd want to jump his bones. This was one of those times.

It wasn't my fault really. He was on the bed, pressed up behind me, and gently running his fingertips up and down my arm.

"Dinner is in thirty minutes. Your mum wanted me to start waking you up now," he said softly, as he kneaded my shoulder and the back of my neck.

"Is the door locked?" I asked quietly, unsure that the door was even closed, let alone locked. I'd have to roll over to check it, and I wasn't gonna move.

He chuckled. "No. Does it need to be?"

I reached behind me and gave his crotch a firm squeeze. "Yes."

He quickly jumped up from the bed and locked the door, as I reached under my dress and pulled off my panties.

"Hurry," I whispered, giggling while he was on his way back to the bed, unbuttoning his pants.

"This is crazy, Zoey."

I didn't give a flying fuck at that point. I needed him right then.

"Where do you want me?" he asked as he arrived back at the bed.

I stood at the edge of the bed and slightly bent over it, bracing myself on my hands.

"Oh fuck yes," he growled as he lifted up my dress and slid his fingers inside me from behind to make sure I was ready for him.

"Hard and fast, please . . . I'm already halfway there," I teased as he pulled his fingers out and thrust into me, with his pants around his knees. *Oh, yes. That's incredible.*

Less than ten minutes later, we were done and cleaning up in the guest bathroom. My man would go for hours or just a few minutes if necessary, and I loved it.

"Did you have a nice nap, *Mija?*" my mom asked when we came into the kitchen.

Andy gave my hand a knowing squeeze then made a beeline to where the guys were in the other room. He didn't want to have to make eye contact with my mom because he thought she would know what we had just done. Chicken-shit.

"It was wonderful," I said without skipping a beat. "Sorry I fell asleep and didn't help out very much."

She glanced up at me and smiled. I don't think she suspected anything, but she wasn't letting on if she did.

"It's okay. I remember those pregnancy days, Zoey."

Later that night after we went home and got Hamish and Sarah settled in the guest room, Andy and I went to bed and laughed hysterically about our little tryst at my parents' house. He decided we needed to do it again, this time at our place so he could take his time with me. Of course, I said yes.

Chapter Twenty

Zoey

December 2012

I woke up late from a restful night's sleep with the sun shining through the window in the bedroom of the apartment above the shop. Andy and I had been here only a short time, but he made sure everything we moved over from the loft was put away.

Andy, my dad, and my brothers packed everything we owned, with the exception of anything we absolutely needed, and moved it to a storage building so the renovations could get underway on our place.

Eyes closed, I laid there silently listening to Andy while he cooked breakfast. I smelled French toast and something else. It was something sweet, and floral, to be exact. Slowly, I opened my eyes, and sitting on the nightstand next to the bed was a beautiful pot of very fragrant, pink and white Stargazer lilies.

He knew I didn't like flower bouquets because they always died, so when he did buy me flowers, he always bought me something I could plant and enjoy every season when they bloomed.

After I rolled from the bed, I took a shower and dressed in some of my man's pajama pants and his All Blacks hoody. It was my birthday darn it, and I wanted to be comfortable. It was a bit chilly in the apartment, so I stuck my feet into my fuzzy slippers and headed out to the kitchen, turning up the thermostat on the way.

I snuck up behind Andy who was at the stove flipping a piece of French toast in a pan. I slid my arms around his waist and kissed his bare back.

"Good morning." I kissed him again, rested my cheek on his back, and breathed him in. He was always so warm, and always smelled good. It comforted me like nothing else could.

He set the spatula aside and turned around, wrapping me in his arms.

"Happy birthday, Beautiful," he said as he hugged me tightly. "You're supposed to be asleep still so I can bring you brekkie in bed."

I raised up on my toes and kissed him. "Thank you for the lilies, and I can go back to bed if you want me to."

He smiled. "You would do that for me? Just because I wanted to bring you brekkie in bed on your birthday?"

"Yes. I will do anything for you, and if you want to bring me *brekkie* in bed on my birthday . . . I guess I'm going back to bed."

Before heading back to the bedroom, I kissed him lightly on the lips, and placed another kiss on his tattooed chest.

As I walked down the hallway I heard him holler, "I love you, birthday girl!" I grinned and shook my head. *God that man makes me happy.*

After propping myself up against the pillows in our bed, I turned on my iPod and listened to music while I waited for my sexy husband to deliver me breakfast. A few minutes later, he walked in carrying a tray and set it over my legs. I noticed something white and blue that looked a whole lot like a Dutch Bros. cup.

I eyed Andy curiously. I hadn't drank coffee in months.

"Don't worry, it's decaf," he reassured me.

I wanted to give him a thank you kiss for the surprise coffee, but the tray and my belly were in the way. "Come here," I said and leaned as close as possible toward him.

He came in for a kiss, then picked up my fork and knife and began cutting up my French toast for me.

Seriously? I giggled. "Wow, I'm really getting spoiled today, huh?"

He nodded, smiling, and continued cutting up my food. When he was finished, he handed me my fork.

"What, you're not going to feed me too?" Jokingly, I folded my arms across my chest and frowned.

He snatched the fork out of my hand and stabbed a piece of French toast with it. Once he held it up to my mouth, and I tried to take the bite, he jerked it back and shoved it into his mouth.

"Okay, smartass . . . you're never allowed to feed me again on my birthday. Last year you ate all my dessert."

"Zoey, you couldn't even hold the spoon because you were so drunk. You're lucky you got to eat any of your dessert." He chuckled at the memory of our dinner at the Mexican restaurant and handed my fork back to me.

As I ate my breakfast, I fed him too. I even shared a few sips of my coffee with him.

"You know," he said, "this brekkie was supposed to be for you."

I shrugged and fed him another bite of French toast. After he refused to eat any more, I finished off the rest of the food on my plate. He set my half-full coffee cup on my nightstand and picked up the tray to take it back to the kitchen.

"Stay right here," he said. "I have pressies for you."

I smiled and hoped he would never stop using Kiwi words and phrases. It was adorable when he said them, and I wanted him to teach them to our children.

Andy came back in with a medium sized gift bag and a tiny blue gift bag from Tiffany & Co. He set them on the bed in front of me, then walked back out of the room and returned with a plate of French toast for himself.

"Open those while I eat," he said as he tipped his chin toward the gift bags.

Of course, I opened the Tiffany bag first and pulled out a small, flat box. Luckily, it wasn't a ring box. I had a feeling he might spend too much money on my birthday or buy me that ridiculously expensive ring he had picked out before.

I was pleasantly surprised when I opened the box and found a silver necklace with a heart shaped pendant. Also hanging on the chain was a tiny, key charm.

"It's beautiful, thank you. Is this the key to your heart?"

Andy set his plate down and stood to put the necklace on me. "No, smartass. After I gave you my heart, I threw *that* key away so you would keep my heart forever."

Sometimes the things that came out of his mouth cracked me up. "You're such a cheeseball, but I still love you," I joked.

He chuckled. "I say stupid shit like that to keep that gorgeous smile on your face."

Yep, that made me smile. Again.

When he was finished with my necklace, I pulled him onto the bed and held him close.

"I swear I'll keep your heart forever, my love, and guard it with my life."

He pulled back and pressed his forehead to mine. "I love you, Zoey. Happy birthday."

He kissed me and sat back down to eat, handing me my next present. I pulled the tissue paper out of the bag and took out a box wrapped in pale, pink paper and silvery-gray, satin ribbon. I tugged the ribbon loose and carefully pulled off the paper.

Inside the wrapping paper was an expensive looking digital camera. I looked at him inquisitively. We had never even talked about cameras before.

"You can't keep using your cell phone to take pictures once Hannah is born," he explained. "It records videos too and has a couple different lenses."

I loved it. He was Mr. Practical, getting me a camera.

I rose to my knees and walked across the bed to where he was sitting. "Thank you so much. I love everything. Especially you."

I hugged him, and then kissed his delicious lips. He tasted like French toast, powdered sugar, and . . . Andy.

"Mmm, you taste scrumptious," I said and kissed him again.

He set his empty plate on the nightstand then took the bags and camera off the bed.

"I have one more for you," he said with a smirk as he dropped his jeans and boxers to the floor. He pulled the hoody over my head, then rid me of the rest of my clothes and gave me one hell of a birthday present.

After my wonderful birthday morning, I was unfortunately, needed at the store. Andy had a meeting at the contractor's office, to go over a few final plans. I dressed in maternity jeans, and one of Andy's James Racing T-shirts since none of mine fit me anymore.

Jerry, one of the guys who worked at our parts desk helping customers, had called me because they were having an issue with one of the computers. I fixed the computer eventually and took a stroll to the warehouse to check out the progress on the installation of the new security doors Andy had insisted upon.

The back warehouse had no windows, but in the store, new security doors in addition to windows were being installed too. I talked with the men who were working on the doors for a few minutes then made my way up to the front of the store.

"Zoey, do you mind if I run to the bathroom real quick?" Jerry asked as I came through the back door from the storeroom.

Jerry was the only one in the store as our cashier Tara was on her lunch break, but she would be back any time. "Yeah, Jerry, go ahead. I can handle it out here."

I walked up and down the aisles to see if anything needed to be done. I restocked a row of brake cleaner, turned around to take the empty box to the back room, and ran smack into Rob.

He was carrying a bouquet of flowers.

"What are you doing here, Rob?"

He backed up and looked me over, shock and anger overtaking his face. "You're pregnant?"

"No shit, Sherlock." I was not in the mood for his crap, especially on my birthday. "You need to leave before Andy gets back. If he sees you here, it's only going to end badly."

He smirked. "What's that *Aussie* piece of shit gonna do?"

I shook my head not bothering to correct Rob about where Andy was actually from. "Fine, I'll go call my brothers. All four of them will be here in about one minute."

I turned my back on him to use the phone at the parts desk to call over to the shop.

His fingers curled around my wrist and he squeezed hard, jerking me back toward him.

"Don't you fucking dare, you bitch," he growled.

Whoa, what the fuck? He had never, *ever* laid a hand on me before, so I was in complete shock at his outburst.

It was then that I took a good look at him, and noticed how thin he'd become since I last saw him. His face was so close to mine, I could smell the rotten stench of his breath. His black hair was stringy, and dirty. I noticed his teeth and gums were rotting, and he had nasty sores on his face.

He's been doing meth. I would recognize those signs anywhere.

"*Rob!*" I screeched as he twisted my wrist even more, and fiery pain burned up my arm to my shoulder. "Let go! You're hurting me!"

He moved closer to my face, so that every time he talked, little drops of his spit hit me.

"You fucking cunt," he growled. "You think you're so much better than me now, don't you?"

I tried wrenching my arm free, but he gripped it tighter. *Fuck that hurts.*

My wrist met its rotation limit, but Rob didn't stop twisting. He continued turning my entire arm until my body was doubling over from the pain. If he twisted any more, I would end up on the floor.

He bent down and got in my face again. "I should burn this fucking place to the ground with you in it."

What the hell? I was terrified. I could feel my body trembling from the adrenaline pumping through my veins.

Rob twisted my arm one more time, and I had no choice but to drop to my knees. I was bent over with my arm wrenched up behind me, and my face almost touching the floor. I cried out in pain. I didn't think my arm could take much more.

He finally let go of me, and that's when I assumed he saw my wedding rings.

"You fucking *married* that guy?" He threw the bouquet of flowers, hitting me in the head.

Petals and leaves broke free from them, littering my hair and the floor around me. I nodded but stayed on the floor. I didn't know what else to do. The man was off his fucking rocker right then, and I didn't want to piss him off more.

"Rob, *please*," I said quietly. "You need to get help. Why are you doing this?"

Where was Jerry? Couldn't he hear what was going on?

"I came here to talk to you Zoey, to tell you happy birthday," he hissed. "I miss you . . . and I come here, and I find you like . . . this!"

He glared down at me, then my stomach. His face contorted in disgust. "That should be *my* baby, not his." He looked me directly in the eyes and yelled, "You killed *my* baby, Zoey!"

What the fuck was he talking about? He knew I'd had a miscarriage even though he hadn't even bothered going to the hospital when I had gone to the ER.

He stood and paced furiously, running his hands through his greasy hair. "How could you do this to me?" he growled and stopped to glare down at me.

What was he talking about? I hadn't seen or heard from him in months. I knew from the experience with my birth mom that people who were so far gone on meth, tended to get paranoid and thought people were out to get them. He must be at that point.

The bell dinged as someone opened the front door, so I screamed for help. Rob stopped pacing, reached down, and grabbed a handful of my hair, yanking me up toward him.

"Shut the fuck up!" he screamed in my face, spitting all over me again in the process.

I smacked at his hands and tried to pull them out of my hair. I felt and heard the strands being ripped from my scalp.

Rob loosened his grip and pushed me back toward the floor. I twisted my body and landed on my side. I instinctively wrapped my arms around my stomach to protect Hannah.

He brought his right foot back, then swung his leg forward to kick me. Right at the last second, I brought my knees up, so I was in the fetal position when his foot connected. I successfully shielded Hannah with my legs and arms, but ended up being kicked on the shins instead of the stomach.

In the next instant, our little spitfire cashier, Tara, launched herself at Rob, and screamed for help. She wielded a tire iron in her hands and hit him in the back with it as hard as she could.

While she wailed on him, I scrambled to my feet, grabbed a can of brake cleaner, and sprayed him in the face with it. He howled in pain as he blindly wrestled with Tara. He backed up a step and she hit him again.

Rob tried to shield himself from Tara's swinging, but it wasn't working out so well for him. She landed two more hard hits to his arms before he ran through the store and out the front door, falling down the steps in the process.

A split second later, Jerry, and the men who were installing the security doors came barreling through the back door. Everything happened so fast, Rob was already gone by the time they ran into the store.

I was lucky Tara came in when she did. Who knew what Rob would have done next.

"Tara," I blubbered. "Tara . . . Thank you."

She dropped the tire iron, ran to me, and escorted me to the parts desk to sit down. I heard someone on the phone calling 911.

"Are you hurt?" I asked Tara.

"No. I'm fine. Zoey, you need to sit down, okay? Don't worry about me."

I sat down on a chair someone brought out from the break room. I was shaking uncontrollably, and my wrist was on fire. I didn't know how much time had passed, but I heard sirens and they were getting closer.

"He tried kicking me in the stomach, Tara," I cried, realizing he could have *killed* Hannah. *Oh God, he tried to kill my baby.*

Tara hugged me. "Shh, Zoey," she said quietly as she rubbed her hand up and down on my back. "Try to stay calm, please. The cops just pulled up."

Everything turned to complete chaos when all four of my brothers came pushing through the back door.

"Zoey?" Jeremy knelt down on the floor next to my chair. "Are you alright? What the hell happened?"

I threw my arms around my brother's neck. "Rob," I sobbed. "He attacked me . . . Jer . . . he tried to kick me in the stomach." I couldn't stop crying.

Jeremy put his arms around my shoulders and under the backs of my knees and lifted me up. He sat down on the chair with me on his lap and let me cry on his shoulder.

Chapter Twenty-One

Andy

Zoey was going to be so pissed at me. After my meeting with the contractor to go over a few changes to the loft, I stopped at the Chevy dealership and ordered her a brand new Chevy Tahoe for Christmas. Her Audi was safe, but small, and I didn't like the thought of her driving around with a new baby inside. Memories of the truck hitting my family's car would always haunt me because I had seen the truck veer across the lane just before hitting us, smashing our mid-sized car into the size of a small car.

On my drive home, I had to pull off to the side of the road three times to let police cruisers and an ambulance pass. Flashing lights and screaming sirens flew by, then once the way was clear, I pulled back onto the road with the rest of the traffic. When I turned onto my street, the scene in front of me unfolded in slow motion.

The police cars and ambulance that had passed me earlier were all parked around the store, lights still flashing. *Zoey. Oh fuck, please let her be okay.* I floored the gas pedal and drove as fast as I could toward the store, only stopping long enough at the stop signs to make sure nobody was in the intersections. At the side of the building, I crammed my truck in park, not bothering to shut it off, or close the door when I exited. My feet were on the ground and running toward the entrance as my brain caught up to the scene surrounding me.

Running up the wheelchair ramp along the side of the store, I made a sharp right and ran into two policemen standing guard at the door.

The two men took a defensive stance. One took hold of my biceps, and the other pushed one hand against my chest while his other hand went to his gun, unsnapping the holster in the process.

"This is my store, let me in!"

"Sir, this is a crime scene. What is your name?"

"Andy Tate. My wife Zoey and I own this building. Where is she? Is she inside? Is she okay?" I pushed against the officers, attempting to look through the windows to see if Zoey was inside. *He said crime scene . . . Oh fuck, oh fuck. Please don't let that mean how it sounds.*

"You're the husband?"

"Yes, now let me inside so I can check on my wife."

I lunged, wedging myself between them enough to push the door open part way. "Let me the fuck inside!" I yelled straining against their hold. Suddenly, I was tackled from behind, thrown to the concrete, and my arms wrenched behind me. The handcuffs were seconds from being slapped around my wrists when I heard Zoey's sweet voice call out to them to let me in.

Oh thank God she's okay . . . My thoughts instantly raced from Zoey to Hannah. *Fuck! She has to be okay too.* "Please, let me in to check my wife and baby."

The officers didn't let me up until they'd taken my wallet out of my back pocket and called in to their dispatch to verify my identity. Once they had confirmation of who I was, they released me and I ran inside the store.

Over the tops of the aisles, I saw a small gathering of people near the parts desk. When I reached them, Zoey was sitting in a chair on Jeremy's lap. His arms were holding her protectively and she was crying into the crook of his neck. My heart hammered in my chest at the site. *Fuck, she's hurt.*

I ran to them and dropped to my knees, sliding the last few feet across the floor to a stop next to her. "Zoey, are you okay? Is Hannah okay?" Without waiting for an answer, I anxiously checked her over myself. She looked unhurt physically for the most part, but there was a nasty looking bruise coming to the surface on her wrist, and her hair was a tangled mess with what appeared to be flower petals in it. *What the fuck happened?*

"Sir, please step back so we can do our job," said one of the paramedics.

I moved aside, but took hold of my wife's hand and dropped to my knees beside her.

"Andy, thank God you're here. I was so scared."

"What happened? Were we robbed? Are you sure you're both alright?" The words that came from her mouth next shocked the hell out of me.

"No," she said. "We weren't *robbed,* but it was Rob who did this."

I dropped her hand and started pacing. I glanced down at Jeremy and met his eyes. They bore the same lethal glare as mine. *Shit, no wonder the cops acted the way they did when I arrived.* Since they knew her ex-husband had attacked her they had automatically assumed I was him when I told them I was her husband.

"Motherfucker," I growled. "I'm gonna kill that fucker when I find him."

"Not if I find him first," Jeremy muttered. "Either way, he's fucked."

Zoey grabbed my hand when I paced by and stopped me. "Please calm down, you two. You're making me anxious."

At the same time, Jeremy and I both apologized to her.

"Where the hell was everyone? How could this have happened?" I asked to nobody in particular.

Jeremy answered for Zoey. "Tara was at lunch, Josh is off today, and Jerry took a break. Now they're all in the break room with my brothers. I wasn't leaving Z out here alone so I don't know the whole story yet. I was holding on to her until you got here."

"Thanks, man." I didn't know what else to say to him. He was very protective of her and I appreciated him staying with her.

The paramedic finished examining her shins and picked up her arm to inspect her wrist.

She winced from the pain. "Ouch," she said quietly and looked up at the paramedic. "That really hurts. Do you think it's broken?"

"I don't think so, but we should take you in to get an x-ray."

She shook her head. "I'll have my husband drive me to the ER after we're done here with the police."

"Are you sure?" he asked. "You'll need to have your baby checked out too. You're *positive* he didn't make contact with your stomach when he kicked you?"

"He *kicked* you, Zoey?" My blood was ablaze with anger and worry.

"Yes, but we're okay." Her eyes were pleading for me to believe her. "I pulled my legs up in front of my stomach. That's why my shins are so bruised."

I knelt in front of her and laid my hands on her stomach.

"Just my legs, Andy, I promise. He didn't hit my stomach at all."

I was about to go ballistic from this news, and I frowned at her. "You're going to the hospital, *now*."

She placed her hands on mine and nodded. "Let's go then."

I sat right where I was until the paramedics brought in a stretcher and helped her onto it. If she said she was all right physically, I believed her. But, she needed an x-ray for her wrist, and I needed to see my baby girl on the sonogram screen with my own eyes.

The police finally let everyone out of the break room, and her brothers came into the store. Tara already told them what had happened, and she and Jerry were released to go home by the police once their statements had been taken.

An officer came over to talk to Zoey as she sat on the stretcher. He introduced himself as Officer Kyle Sherman. He didn't look like he was any older than Zoey. He had sandy brown hair, cut in the standard cop style, and determined, hazel eyes.

"Mrs. Tate," he said, "I'll meet you over at the hospital to get your statement if that's alright with you. I'd rather they get you checked out first."

She nodded and said that was fine, then they wheeled her out the door with me walking alongside the stretcher. Once she was settled in the back of the ambulance, I sat down next to her on the bench.

With one hand, I rubbed Zoey's rounded stomach while the fingers of my other hand laced through hers. "Are you sure you're both okay?"

"Yes."

She scooted over as far as she could on the stretcher and held her arms out to me. I would never deny her need to touch me if it comforted her. I'd made too many mistakes in the past and wouldn't repeat them. When she'd been knocked unconscious outside of her dance class, and ended up in the hospital for two days, I'd refused to touch her; afraid I would hurt her worse. I eased down onto the narrow stretcher next to her, pulling her into my arms.

"Please tell me everything that happened."

So she did. A smile pulled at the corners of my mouth when she told me how she sprayed Rob in the face with brake cleaner and how Tara beat the hell out of him with a tire iron. I'd be giving Tara a raise for that.

While sitting behind a curtain in the ER, I heard the familiar voice of Officer Sherman ask a nurse where Zoey was. He came and interviewed her, then took a few pictures of her injuries while we waited for a doctor.

"Excuse me," a deep manly voice said from the other side of the curtain. "Officer Sherman? May I have a word with you, please?"

"Give me just a minute," he said. He stood and pulled the curtain aside.

As soon as he closed the curtain, Zoey lifted her shirt, placing her hands over the swell of her stomach. She smiled down at herself the way she always did when Hannah was kicking. I placed one hand on top of hers and she shifted hers on top of mine, then slid them to where our baby girl was moving.

"Are you sure he didn't hit her, Zoey?" I asked, then leaned over and kissed her stomach. I pressed my cheek to her skin, and my tiny girl gave me several kicks to my face. They were as strong as ever, giving me the reinforcement that she really was okay.

"Yes, I'm positive. He would have had to kick through my shins, thighs and my arms. Watch, I'll show you what I did."

Since she was lying on her side, I sat back up so she could move. She demonstrated how she pulled up her arms and legs to shield herself and Hannah. I took her extremely bruised wrist in my hand and kissed it. I could clearly see where Rob's hand had been on her wrist from the way the bruise was forming.

It looked like a grotesque, twisted handprint.

"Mrs. Tate, may I come in?" It was Officer Sherman again. I pulled the curtain back and let him in.

"Good news," he said to Zoey. "We've just arrested your ex-husband."

"That was quick," she said.

"The gentleman who came to get me was a hospital security guard. One of the nurses pulled him aside and said a man was in the ER saying he'd been attacked, but his story wasn't adding up. He's being treated right now for possible broken ribs, a broken arm, and brake cleaner in his eyes and face."

Officer Sherman winked at her. "You and your friend Tara really did a number on him."

That dirty motherfucker was in the same hospital ER as us and instantly I bristled. I wanted to search every single exam room until I found him then beat the hell out of him. Zoey must have noticed my body language change to that of a caged animal because she took my hand and drew me closer. My tension decreased and I sat down on the exam table next to her.

"I think I've got everything I need," Officer Sherman said. "I'll be in touch soon. You have a tough wife there, Mr. Tate." He shook my hand then turned and left us alone.

After the doctor examined Zoey and Hannah, and gave them the all clear, we took a taxi home since we'd ridden to the hospital in an ambulance. I helped her shower so she could scrub away what she referred to as "Rob's nastiness" then sent her to bed. Once I called her family to tell them she was home and all was well, I slid into bed behind her.

"I'm so sorry I wasn't there to protect you and Hannah, Zoey." I curved my body around hers, sliding my arm over her hip to rest my hand on her belly.

"I was so scared, Andy." She sniffled and cried, her body shaking. "I'm fine now that it's all over with, but when I realized that he could have killed Hannah, I was terrified."

I inched in closer to her and kissed her hair. "You are amazing. You protected yourself and our daughter. You are so brave and strong, Beautiful." Holding her and running my fingers through her hair, finally calmed her down.

Even though Zoey assured me that she was fine, what that piece of shit Rob had done to her was going to get to her at some point. I wanted to be prepared for when it did. I would be sure to call Dr. Jensen to schedule an appointment for her as soon as her office opened the next day. I felt like a failure for not being there to protect her and Hannah.

Thank God for Tara. If she hadn't come back from lunch when she did . . . Fuck, I didn't even want to think about what Rob could have done to Zoey. I wanted to kill the little fucker for the pain he had caused her, but that would take me away from my wife and child and I wouldn't risk that for anything. I would just make sure he'd never have another chance to get anywhere near her.

Finally, after I rubbed her back for a while, Zoey drifted off to sleep. I pulled the blankets up around her and held her tighter. I would never let anything happen to her again, no matter what I had to do.

Chapter Twenty-Two

I'm sitting in a cold, hard metal chair, surrounded by my family. The frigid, dead air of winter is chilling me to the bone. Andy is standing off to the side, by himself. He won't even look at me. I stare down at the wad of tissue in my hands, bright white against the black of my dress. Tiny flecks of lint from the tissue stand out on my dress.

"Mija," my mom whispers as she takes my hand in hers. "It's time."

I gather what strength I have left and stand, my dad links his arm through mine to balance me. Glancing over to where Andy is standing, I find he is no longer there.

My mom and dad walk on either side of me, up to the tiny white casket that holds my precious daughter inside.

"I can't do this," I whisper as hot tears stream down my cold face. "I can't let her go."

The other mourners around us leave as the casket is lowered slowly into the cold ground. I search for Andy. We need to do this together, but I can't find him. Why did he leave me again?

I stare down at the casket as it settles at the bottom of the hole.

Oh God, please help me. How did this happen?

I toss a Stargazer lily into the grave on top of the casket. I don't even know where the lily came from, but I wonder if the stars burn brighter where my baby girl's spirit is. I turn to walk the few feet back to my chair, but it is gone.

All the chairs are gone. I don't remember seeing my parents leave, but as I look around, I am completely alone. It was as if nobody has even been there.

I turn back to my daughter's grave. It is already filled in with dirt, and tiny sprouts of new grass have popped up through the soil. *How long have I been here? What is going on? I am so confused.*

I feel the urge to leave. As I walk away, I think I hear a baby crying. I turn back to the grave. The crying is getting louder.

She is still alive, and we buried her. She is screaming for me.

I run back to the grave and fall on my hands and knees, my breath coming in gasps. She is still screaming.

I tear at the fresh dirt with my bare hands. I am screaming for help, but nobody is coming. I dig, and dig at the dirt as I beg someone, anyone, to help me.

Suddenly, Andy is right next to me.

"Zoey, no!" he yells. "Stop, you're going to hurt yourself!"

He is trying to stop me.

"She's screaming! Can't you hear her?" I cry, completely hysterical. Why isn't he doing anything?

He grabs at my hands.

I slap and push at him, to make him stop grabbing at me. "Help me!" I scream at him.

He grips my arms and gives me a good shake to get my attention. "Zoey please . . . stop. Please," he begs again in a loud whisper.

Why isn't he helping me?

I shake him loose and return to scraping away the dirt. He lunges at me. I slap him and claw at him.

He pulls me into a bear hug to pin my flailing arms to my sides. "Zoey," he murmurs soothingly in my ear. "It's only a dream, please wake up. Beautiful, please, please wake up."

The word *dream* sunk in through my panic, and I suddenly felt his strong arms around me. His voice was soft and comforting in my ear as he whispered that everything was okay and that he loved me.

My eyes shot open, and I was in our bedroom, in the apartment above the shop. The lights were on, and I was sitting straight up on the bed, Andy beside me, with his arms wrapped firmly around me.

His arms were pinning mine to my sides, and his left leg was thrown over my legs, pinning them down too. I was completely immobilized, my throat raw from screaming.

"What the hell is going on?" I cried, as I struggled to free myself.

"Shh, Zoey," he whispered in my ear. "It was just a dream. Can I let go of you now?"

I could barely hear him over the thumping of my heart resonating in my ears. I nodded and he released his hold on me.

I was scared to death because the dream felt so real, I still thought my daughter was dead. I slowly looked down, expecting to see a flat stomach, but instead, I found my round, pregnant belly.

My daughter was still there, unharmed, growing inside me. I sobbed with relief.

Suddenly feeling like I was going to be sick, I jumped off the bed and ran toward the bathroom. I didn't make it. I collapsed on my knees in the hallway right outside our bedroom door and threw up all over the floor. I sat back on my heels, just as Andy crouched beside me.

"Are you okay?" he asked quietly as he rubbed my back.

"I don't know," I cried. I was so scared and confused.

"Come on let's get you back in bed," he said and helped me stand.

Finally, I looked up at him. Expressions of panic, concern, and confusion were all over his pale face. He had scratch marks on the side of his neck, and he was bleeding.

"*Nooo, no, no, no,*" I cried, as I reached up to his neck. "Oh God, did I do that to you?"

"Don't worry about it." He caught my hand and ushered me back to our bed. "Get back in bed and tell me what happened."

Andy sat on the bed first, propped up against the pillows and headboard, and patted the mattress between his thighs, motioning for me to sit. I sat on the bed, and pulled the covers back up over us as I reclined against his chest.

He took my hands and placed them on my belly, with his hands over mine. "Zoey, everything is alright now," he said softly as he kissed the side of my head. "Please tell me what happened."

I glanced over at the clock on the nightstand and found that it was three-thirty in the morning. Everything from the previous day came flooding back to me. Then my nightmare came back to me, and I started crying.

It took me a while to tell Andy what my nightmare was about, because it was so horrible. The entire time I talked, he sat patiently and listened.

Hannah began moving around as I told him the story. It was amazing to feel her moving after my unbearable nightmare. She was okay and so was I, and Andy was here with me. The two loves of my life were still right here with me.

"I'm so sorry." I sat forward and looked over my shoulder at him. He was still pale, as if he were physically ill from listening to what happened in my dream. I needed to clean the floor and clean his scratches. I threw the blankets off to get up.

"What are you doing?" he asked, and followed me from the bed.

"Cleaning up my messes."

I walked through the doorway and glanced down as I sidestepped the puddle in the hallway. I'd only thrown up liquid. Fuck. I hadn't eaten anything since breakfast yesterday. Not good, Zoey.

Quickly, I grabbed a towel from the bathroom cabinet, ran it under the faucet at the sink, and went back into the hall.

Andy stood in the doorway to the bedroom and held his hand out for the wet towel.

I shook my head. "I'll do it." I wasn't going to let him clean up my puke.

"Zoey, please," he said, "let me do it for you."

I sighed. "I didn't get to eat after breakfast yesterday. Can you fix me something while I clean this up?"

He'd never deny that request because he always made sure I ate and took care of Hannah and myself. He stepped past me into the hallway without another word.

After he went to the kitchen, I got on my knees and cleaned the floor. When I was done, I rinsed the towel in the bathtub until I was sure all the puke was gone then hung it on the edge of the tub to dry. I brushed my teeth, cleaned myself up, and found the first aid kit.

In the kitchen, I took out antiseptic wipes and antibiotic cream to clean Andy's scratches. I could not believe what I had done. He'd only been trying to keep me from hurting Hannah, or myself.

Andy set a plate with a sandwich on it in front of me, and went to get me a glass of water. He sat down in the chair next to me. I was sick to my stomach at the helpless expression on his distraught face. Not only did he have the claw marks on his neck, but he had scratches running down his forearms too.

"Andy," I whimpered, and buried my face in my hands. "I'm so sorry I hurt you."

He placed his hand on my cheek to comfort me. "I'm fine, Beautiful. Are you sure you're okay?"

I didn't answer him. I definitely wasn't okay.

Kneeling on the floor next to him, I cleaned his wounds. I was horrified and wept the entire time, but he sat silently and let me do it. He knew I needed to, because I would never forgive myself, if I couldn't make it right. After I finished, I crawled onto his lap and he just held me.

"Zoey," he said quietly, getting my attention. "Please, you need to eat."

He was right. I felt like a horrible mother and wife at that moment, but I couldn't bring myself to leave the comfort and safety of his arms, so I stayed on his lap to be close to him. Slowly, I ate the entire sandwich. I didn't even taste it. There was no way I was going back to sleep after my nightmare, so I sat on the couch and stared off into space for a while.

I was definitely taking the day off from work to get an emergency appointment with Dr. Jensen. I had completely lost it because of the nightmare, and in the process, I had physically assaulted the one person I never wanted to hurt.

Sometime during my space out session, Andy came and sat on the couch with me, covering us both with a blanket.

"Andy," I whispered. "I'm so sorry for hitting you. I didn't mean to do it."

He took my hand and laced his fingers with mine. "I know. It's not your fault, Zoey. You almost fell off the bed. I didn't know how else to keep you from hurting yourself or Hannah."

"Thank you," I replied as he wrapped me in the comfort of his strong arms.

Chapter Twenty-Three

Zoey

The next several days passed without any more nightmares. My bruises slowly faded, and Andy's scratches healed. I went to a few appointments with Dr. Jensen to talk about the attack and my dream. Andy attended them as well. He was worried about me, and we both thought it would be good for him to sit in on the sessions.

Rob was still in jail and charged with simple battery. Andy was in a rage that he wasn't being charged with attempted murder. I didn't blame Andy, and I fully agreed with him. Rob did try to kick a pregnant woman in the stomach.

Andy went to every single court hearing and frequently spoke to Officer Sherman. They were actually becoming good friends. The only reason Rob was still in jail was that nobody would bail him out. Not even his family.

I had frequent visits from Tara and we had bonded over our tag team defense from Rob. I hadn't left our apartment much since the attack, other than to go to and from work and I hadn't even started my Christmas shopping because of it.

We had an appointment with Dr. Stewart, who confirmed that baby Hannah was growing right on schedule and would arrive toward the end of February. The renovations were under way on the loft.

In the form of destruction, that is.

The construction crew knocked down internal walls, while windows, wiring, and plumbing were being replaced. The bottom floor had already been fitted with new windows and security doors. We were waiting for the installation of the new alarm system.

It would be months before we would move back in, so we would be in the cramped, one bedroom apartment over the shop when Hannah was born. However, the three of us would be together, and that was all that mattered to us.

Because I'd been feeling a bit claustrophobic being cooped up in the apartment, I asked Andy to take me shopping for Christmas, and to shop for things for the baby too. Jess and Sasha were throwing me a baby shower after the first of the year, and I needed to register for gifts like they'd asked me to.

We took Andy's truck and went shopping. We bought toys for Jake and Alex, and I had a hard time leaving the store without buying too many cute, girly things for Mya.

We had quite a bit of fun scanning everything for the baby shower registry too. Andy put himself in charge of registering for safety equipment, and of course, he went nuts with it. I was surprised that he didn't want to put in padded walls.

A week before Christmas, I decided to go shopping one afternoon by myself to buy Andy's Christmas presents. He decided to go shopping too since he said he hadn't had time to buy me anything for Christmas either.

He had mentioned on a few occasions how small my Audi was, and wondered how we were going to fit in a car seat and a baby, along with all of her things. I threatened him with no sex for a month if he went out and bought me a new car. Of course, he teasingly laughed at me and said I could never resist him.

He was right because he knew I'd never be able to refuse him.

He mumbled something about not buying me a new car before he kissed me goodbye.

The way he said the word *car,* I knew he was up to something.

Now that I knew he had all that money, I had no idea what I would get him for Christmas. Technically, he could buy whatever he wanted, whenever he wanted. That made it so much more difficult for me to shop for him.

I ended up sticking with the usual man-type gifts. I bought him some new clothes, cologne, and even found some pretty lingerie for myself to wear for him. I'd have to wait until after Hannah arrived to wear any of it, but I knew he would love it.

After spending hours shopping, I was exhausted and anxious to get home to make dinner. I stashed all the bags in my trunk and headed home.

When I pulled onto our street, I came to a roadblock. Looking around, I saw fire department barricades blocking off the street. What the hell? I rolled down my window and smelled smoke in the air. It had a funky chemical smell to it.

Shifting into reverse, I backed up my car and turned it around in an attempt to get to my place using a different route. That street was blocked too. *Son of a bitch.* I was tired and hungry from shopping and just wanted to go home.

I pulled out my cell to call Andy and let him know I couldn't get home because the streets were blocked. He didn't answer. I couldn't even see the shop or the store from the street I was on because there were too many trees around.

There was one other road I could try to get home, so again, I reversed my car and flipped a U-turn. The next street wasn't blocked yet, so I drove toward my place. The closer I came to home, the more worried I became. I was getting near enough I could see the smoke was coming from the area right over the store and our loft. I sped up, but once I was closer, I found the road was blocked. I parked on the street and hurried out to the barricade to talk to a police officer who was standing guard.

"Officer, I need to know if my building is on fire!" I said in a panic. "Can you tell me if it's at James Racing or The Speed Shop?"

He gave me a curt nod. "Let me check for you, ma'am," he said and stepped away, calling someone on his radio.

Shit! I couldn't hear what he was saying.

A few minutes later, he walked back over to me. "Are you Zoey Tate?"

The officer would only know my name if it was my building on fire. *Fuck.* I nodded, as my heart sank.

"Ms. Tate, there was a small fire inside the warehouse at the back of your store. The fire is out. Luckily, it wasn't very big. It was more smoke than fire, so that's good news. The fire department is trying to—"

His radio let out a loud squeal at that moment, and a voice came over it. "We've got a code nine-two-six here, Sergeant. We're gonna need the coroner."

Oh God, someone was dead? Where was Andy? He hadn't answered his phone when I called him. My body shook uncontrollably, so I held my arms around Hannah for comfort.

"Officer, *please* . . . I need to get over there now!" I cried. "My husband might be there."

I prayed harder than I had ever prayed in my life.

Oh God, please don't let it be Andy. Please, God. Oh, no, no, no! We had so much we were looking forward to. *I can't lose him—we can't lose him.*

"Officer, please, I need to get over there," I begged again.

He took pity on me, put his radio up to his mouth, and walked away. I heard him tell someone that Andy might be on the property somewhere.

I pulled my cell out and dialed his number again but he still didn't pick up. I needed to get over there. While the officer had his back to me, I snuck past the barricade and rushed toward my store.

Knowing the area well, I was able to make my way to the back side of the shop before I was grabbed by another cop. Once he realized I was pregnant, he let go of my body, but kept a hold of my arm.

"*Please,*" I begged. "This is my building. I need to find my husband."

I looked over to where Andy's truck was always parked, praying to God it wasn't there, but it was.

My heart sank further when I scanned the crowd of firefighters and policemen but didn't see him anywhere.

Where is he?

My heart was thumping so fast I couldn't catch my breath. I thought I might have a panic attack because I couldn't find him. I was becoming lightheaded, and my knees finally buckled underneath me.

The officer caught me as I went down and helped me sit on the curb.

I was freaking out, thinking about all the plans Andy and I had made. How was I going to raise our daughter on my own? I couldn't do it without him. I didn't *want* to do it without him.

If they told me he was dead, I would want to die right along with him. I hated feeling that way, but I did.

The officer stayed with me after he called a paramedic over to check me out.

I heard through the commotion that the coroner had arrived, and they were going inside my store to pick up the body of a man in his twenties.

As hard as I could, I squeezed my eyes shut and covered my ears so I didn't have to hear them when they told me that my husband was dead. My mind became so overwhelmed, I imagined my body had been lifted from the hard concrete and deposited somewhere safe and comforting.

That's when I took in a deep breath and smelled his cologne. When I opened my eyes, I expected to be sitting on the curb, but I wasn't. I was sitting on someone's lap, tucked into a warm embrace. A paramedic knelt in front of me taking my vitals, and the most beautiful man I had ever seen was beneath me, and whispering in my ear that he loved me.

Andy.

At first, I thought I was dreaming, but then he reached out and pushed my hair off my tear-streaked face.

"Zoey, are you alright?" he asked.

Once the paramedic let go of my wrist, I threw my arms around my husband and hugged him, pressing as close to him as my belly would allow. "I thought you were dead!" I sobbed, shaking uncontrollably.

God, please don't let this be a dream. Please let him be here with me.

"Please don't wake me up this time if I'm dreaming."

I looked at his beautiful face and waited for him to say something. He squeezed me tighter. "Zoey, it's not a dream . . . I'm here . . . I'm right here. I told you I'd never leave you again, and I meant it. *Nothing* can keep me from you."

I grabbed his face hard and kissed him all over it as many times as I could before he started chuckling, and pulled my hands away so he could talk again.

"Zoey, relax. I'm here, Beautiful," he reiterated as he smiled down at me. "Can you try and stand up for me?"

I gave him a nod and he helped me stand up on my wobbly legs. As soon as he stood, I wrapped my arms around him. There was no way I was letting him go.

"Why didn't you answer your phone?" I asked. "I tried to call you when I came to the roadblocks, and then I couldn't find you when I got here."

Andy let go of me and checked his pockets, and came up empty-handed. He tipped his head when he remembered where it was. "Shit. My phone's in my truck on the charger. I'm so sorry I worried you."

The officer who was standing with us received a call on his radio asking if we would be willing to come over and try to identify the body they had taken out of the building.

My mind raced with the thought that it might be any of my brothers inside the building. But why would they be there? It was past closing time, and they would all be at home.

"Zoey, stay here." Andy tried to pry my arms from around him. "I'll go see if I know who it is."

"No way, I am not letting go of you for anything right now." I held him tighter. "I'll go too."

He nodded, knowing better than to argue with me. Besides, I needed to know who had died in our warehouse.

We walked a few feet before he stopped. "Zoey, are you sure you want to go over there?"

No, I'm not sure . . . but I nodded and began walking again.

When I realized I was making it difficult for us both to walk properly, I loosened my hold on him. Once we reached the other side of our store, I let him go briefly and linked my arm with his.

As we followed the officer, my mind began wandering again, and I felt sick to my stomach. Was the person we were to identify going to be burned up? And if they were, would I be able to live with that image in my head for the rest of my life? What if it was one of my brothers? I stopped short, ten feet from the person who was inside the blue body bag, on a stretcher.

"I can't look," I whispered. "What if it's one of my brothers?"

The look in his eyes told me Andy hadn't thought about that. "Stay here."

He pressed a kiss to my hair, and left me to wait for him to come back. I turned my back to the stretcher as I heard the bag being unzipped. I refused to look in that direction. I waited, and a minute later, Andy said he knew the person.

Oh God, who was it? Andy came up behind me and put his arms around me. I didn't turn to face him. I let him hold me as I waited to hear who had died inside our building.

"Zoey, it's Rob," he said quietly.

The next twenty-four hours passed by in mass confusion.

Why was Rob out of jail? Why had nobody told us?

He tried to make good on his promise of burning the place to the ground. At least it had been without me in it like he had threatened.

From his initial examination, the coroner said that Rob had most likely died from smoke inhalation. There were no burns on his body, thank God. I hated the man for what he had done to me, but I didn't want anyone, even him, to suffer like that.

Apparently, he had tried to start the fire with some type of chemical he had found in the back room. We weren't sure of the substance yet, but it was something that caused more smoke than flame. In his rush to get out of the building, he had somehow become confused and overcome by the smoke. He probably couldn't find his way out, because he had never stepped foot inside the warehouse before that day.

The coroner's office was performing toxicology tests to see if he was under the influence of drugs or alcohol when he died. I was ninety-nine percent positive he had been high on meth at the time.

There was a little bit of media attention because of the fire and Rob's death, but it died down after a couple of days. My family thought it was best if we closed the store and the shop until after the new year, giving all our employees paid vacation until we were ready to reopen.

Andy and I decided to go to Sonoma and spend time with Hamish and Sarah after Christmas.

When we returned home after New Year's, Officer Sherman, actually Kyle, since we now considered him a friend, came for a visit. He let us know Rob had been released from jail due to overcrowding. Several offenders that were considered more violent than him had been transferred into the jail to serve time on their sentences. That meant the less dangerous criminals, and those who had been charged with only misdemeanors, as Rob had been, were released until their court dates.

Kyle hadn't been aware because he'd been on vacation for Christmas. Had he known, he would've called us immediately.

Honestly, I didn't want Rob to die, but he would never be able to hurt me again. I finally felt safe and wanted to move on with my life. My life with Andy, Hannah, our families, and friends.

It was the only life I was given and I needed to live it to the fullest. No regrets.

Chapter Twenty-Four

Zoey

March 10, 2013

Officially, I had been in labor for twenty-four hours. According to my doctor's original calculation, Hannah was well over a week late. I was so miserable, and extremely uncomfortable in my own body, I couldn't imagine how cramped *she* was inside of me.

Her amniotic fluid was low, and there was literally no room left for Hannah. I hadn't dilated to anywhere near where I should have, so I was being wheeled into an operating room for a C-section. The doctors had concerns about the cord crimping, or wrapping around her neck because of the lack of room, but her vitals remained strong. As a precaution, they wanted her out of me, and so did I.

Andy and I were more than ready to meet our baby girl.

The previous afternoon, when I had called him over at the shop to tell him my water had broken, I'd been so excited to make that call. All my contractions had come on like they were supposed to, but when we got to the hospital they had stopped. I had hoped for a quick delivery, but apparently, that wasn't going to happen.

Jess was excited because she was supposed to go into the delivery room with Andy and me. She and Noah had just found out they were expecting their first child and she wanted to know what she was in for when she had her baby.

However, since a C-section was in my very near future, Andy was the only person allowed to go in with me.

Because I was overdue when I went in to labor, they kept me at the hospital to monitor Hannah and me. I was grateful for that, because I was scared and nervous. Andy was very attentive as usual, but I could see the constant excitement radiating from him.

He was finally going to be a dad.

Since I chose Hannah's first name, I asked him to choose her middle name. Our little girl's name would be Hannah Lynn Tate. Andy wanted her named after me too, so my middle name was now hers as well. I loved it.

Since Rob's death, we had worked hard on putting bad things from our pasts behind us. Andy and I had made a pact with each other, and decided to start the New Year by concentrating only on the good.

We focused on each other, our family and friends, and Emma. Michelle had sent a brief letter to the shop for Andy, telling him how sorry she was for everything she'd done. She also told him where Emma was buried in San Francisco, and had even sent a baby gift for Hannah.

Andy and I visited little Emma's grave several times, and he was finally able to grieve for his first child. It was difficult the first time we visited, because when we found her headstone, it wasn't Andy's last name chiseled in the granite. It was Michelle's maiden name. Andy felt like Michelle had never even acknowledged the fact that he was Emma's father.

It was as if Emma had never belonged to Andy, even though we knew she did. That very day, after speaking with Michelle, Andy ordered a new headstone, changing Emma's last name to Tate. The next time we visited the cemetery, Andy grieved again at seeing his last name next to hers. Emma Tate existed in his heart and mind, and now, everyone would know she was his daughter.

We let the bad memories go, and cherished only the good memories. We still lived in the apartment over the shop, but the renovations on the loft were moving right along. We both worked at the store as a team when he wasn't working at the shop.

As patiently as possible, we had been waiting for Hannah's arrival.

I was on IV meds for my C-section, so I was a little bit out of it when they wheeled me into the operating room. Andy looked very striking in his scrubs. His blue eyes sparkled with love and excitement, and he had a constant smile on his beautiful face. *Please let our baby girl inherit her daddy's eyes.*

That was my last coherent thought, and the next thing I knew, the doctor was telling me I was going to feel some pressure and pulling from below the sheet blocking my view.

Minutes later, our sweet baby girl was taking her first breath and crying.

It was the most beautiful music I had ever heard in my life.

"You did it, Zoey. She's finally here," Andy whispered in my ear as he wiped tears from my face, then from his own.

He watched as the nursing staff cleaned Hannah off and performed the necessary newborn testing.

"Do you want to cut the cord, daddy?" Doctor Stewart asked happily over Hannah's tiny cries.

Andy smiled and stood from the stool he had been sitting on near my head. "Yes!" he said excitedly. He leaned over to me and kissed my forehead. "I'll be right back, Beautiful. You did great. I'm so proud of you."

"Go meet your daughter, Andy." I smiled at him, sleepy from the drugs.

Several minutes later, he was back at my side, a huge, happy grin on his face.

"Zoey, wait until you see her. She is perfect and beautiful and looks just like you."

I was anxious to see her, but she had to be weighed and measured first. Meanwhile, the doctors worked to get me stitched and stapled back together.

Hannah's continuous crying and adorable little whimpers were music to my ears while Andy stood watching as the nurses tended to our daughter. He relayed her vital statistics back to me as they told him the information. She was seven pounds, six ounces, and twenty-one inches long.

Our girl was here and perfect.

My eyes were heavy, so I closed them for a minute as I listened to my little girl across the room.

"Zoey?" I heard Andy say quietly through the fog in my brain.

My sleepy eyes fluttered open. He was sitting on the same stool he'd vacated earlier and held a tiny little bundle swaddled in pink. I still had tubes and IV's hooked to me so I was unable to touch her until the surgical staff was finished with me, but she was sleeping peacefully in her daddy's arms.

It was, and always would be, the most beautiful image I had ever seen in my life.

"Happy birthday, Hannah Lynn Tate," I whispered to her as tears trickled from my eyes. "She looks so tiny next to you, Andy."

He smiled down at our daughter, his blue eyes full of happy tears.

"Zoey, she's perfect. Thank you so much. This is definitely the best day of our lives. Nothing will *ever* measure up to this very moment. I can't believe that after all these years, I would look at this date as a day that a new life was brought in to my world."

He was right. Twelve years ago to the day, three lives were taken from him and on the same date, twelve years later, our daughter was born. I truly believed that everything happened for a reason, and even though the date had caused Andy such misery before, it now brought him joy and happiness.

Nothing would ever compare to the moment I saw Andy hold our daughter for the first time. I fell more in love with him at that moment, than I ever thought possible. Andy had given me the best gift by giving me my life back, and because of that reason, we had a beautiful baby girl. We loved each other, and we had refused to give up on us.

After what seemed like hours, I was finally in recovery and able to hold our daughter. Like so many times before, I scooted to the side of the bed, and Andy crawled up next to me. We laid there together, just the two of us, and watched our sleeping baby.

The immense love I held for the two people next to me was more than I could have ever imagined. I was so overcome with emotion I was literally unable to form the words to tell my husband how I felt. All I could do was take it in and enjoy it. My life had never been so complete, and it had never held more meaning or purpose.

Over the next few days while I was in the hospital, we had several visitors, and Andy only left us when he had to, then he was back as soon as he could be. Jeremy even got a date with one of the nurses on the maternity floor when he came in to visit me. I had seen her around, and she didn't seem like the type of girl that would settle him down any, but whatever. As long as she was good to him, I had no issues with her.

Once they discharged me from the hospital, I was a bundle of nerves. I worried about taking care of Hannah without the aid of the nursing staff, but I knew Andy would be right there, so that helped.

Luckily, Andy had surprised me on Christmas Day with a new SUV, like I knew he would. He agreed he wouldn't get me a *car,* so he hadn't. I loved my Audi, but he was right, it was not spacious at all. I wanted to keep it, so we did.

My new Chevy Tahoe was more than roomy and the infant seat fit perfectly inside it. I rode in the back seat with Hannah just to watch her when Andy drove us home from the hospital. She was adorable, and I literally could not take my eyes off her. She was all me, but I could see little bits of Andy in her as well.

Once we were home, we settled in to an easy routine of sorts. I could not have asked for a better baby or husband.

While Hannah did look a lot like me, she had Andy's disposition. Like him, she was calm most of the time, but every once in a while, she would throw a little fit and scream her head off. We liked to tease each other about it. I would say that part of her came from him and he would say it came from me. We would have to agree, to disagree on that one.

Both of us were finally at peace with our pasts. We were living each day to the fullest and looking forward to our future.

We had a beautiful life together.

Epilogue

Zoey

August 2014

I sat in the rocking chair and began singing softly to my baby girl. *"Close your eyes . . ."* She loved the song when it played on my iPod, and liked to dance around to it. It was a fairly heavy rock song, so I sang it slowly and quietly to lull her back to sleep. The lyrics were beautiful. Hannah was exactly like me when it came to music. She loved it, and it soothed her as much as it did me.

Once I carefully eased her back into her crib in the bedroom next to ours, I shut her door partway and tiptoed back to my bedroom. After shedding my pajamas, I slipped back into bed next to my gorgeous, sleeping husband, who was lying naked in his usual face plant position. I was still in awe of how he could sleep like that.

He looked too damn sexy when he slept, but I didn't waste any time waking him up so I could take advantage of some alone time with him. I pulled the sheet off him and slipped my naked body on top of his. I kissed his tattooed back between his shoulder blades then reached down and gave his perfect, muscular ass a squeeze.

He groaned sleepily. I lifted myself off him so he could roll over, but as soon as he was on his back, I resumed my position laying on him.

"Happy birthday, Sexy," I said as I reached back down and stroked him. "Are you ready for your first birthday present?"

I kissed his chest and stopped on the way down, to flick my tongue across his nipple.

"So ready," he mumbled.

I continued my descent down his body. His hard cock was ready and waiting for me. I slid down and licked him from base to tip, then took him inside my mouth.

Just over two and a half years after I had snuck into his shower and given him the very first blowjob I'd ever given in my life, I still loved to satisfy him that way. Of course, he never tired of it either—what man would?

I took the base of him in my hand, and began stroking him as I teased him with my tongue. He wound his fingers through my hair, and moaned as I sucked harder. I swirled my tongue around the head, then took him back into my mouth.

"Ah, fuck, Zoey," he groaned.

I sucked, teased, and stroked him until he was panting.

Taking my time with him, since today was his birthday, I let him slip from my mouth, and kissed my way back up his stomach and chest. I positioned myself over him and sank down onto him, then slowly began rocking my hips.

Leaning back and placing my hands on his muscular thighs, his cock rubbed me in all the right places.

He sat up and gripped my hips, right on top of my swirling snowflake tattoos, as he guided me up and down on him, hard and slow. He took my nipple into his mouth, teasing and flicking it with his tongue.

I wrapped my arms around his neck as he continued torturing my breast. My body was tingling with desire for him, and I felt like I was going to combust at any second.

He flicked my nipple again with the tip of his tongue, sucked it hard into his mouth, and then released it. He flipped me over onto my back and began driving into me. I was so aroused already I was going to come.

"Andy, it's *your* birthday . . . Oh that f-feels so good . . ." I moaned as my body began tightening around him.

Andy was already close too, so I scraped my fingernails down his back, causing him to slow his thrusting down. I felt his body stiffen, so I did it again. He continued thrusting into me slowly as he came then collapsed on top of me.

I wrapped my arms around him and held onto him for a few minutes. I wanted to savor the moment with him. "I love you, Andy," I whispered in his ear.

"I love you too, Beautiful." He chuckled as he pulled back and began kissing my neck. "Thank you for the birthday blowjob and the quickie before our girl wakes up for the day."

"The pleasure was all mine, really. It's the first of many birthday presents today." I laughed and smacked him on the ass.

He rolled off me and I turned onto my side, nestling into the crook of his neck. We laid there wrapped in each other and enjoyed our quiet morning. I had a busy day planned for his birthday, so eventually I got up, showered, and began preparing for breakfast.

After Andy had showered, he came into the kitchen, wearing only a pair of white cargo shorts, and carrying a very giggly Hannah. He had gotten her up and ready, dressed in a pale yellow sundress. Her blonde ringlets bounced as he carried her into the kitchen.

He came over to where I was standing at the stove, poaching eggs for our breakfast of eggs Benedict, and kissed me on the cheek. "Good morning, again," he said.

"Mummy!" Hannah called when I turned to kiss them both.

"Good morning, beautiful girl." I kissed her on her head.

Her bright blue eyes sparkled just like her daddy's. I turned back to the stove and poured the scrambled eggs for her into a pan to cook as Andy took her over to the table.

Andy sat down on a chair and laid her on her back on top of his thighs, so her head was resting near his knees. He sent her in to another fit of giggles by blowing raspberries on the bottoms of her bare feet.

She was ticklish too, like her daddy. I chuckled quietly when she began squealing "No daddy!" at him in between her tiny giggles.

I watched my beautiful man play with our daughter, and it made my heart flutter in my chest. I could watch him with her every second, of every day. He was very devoted and loved his daughter more than life itself.

He had an 'H' tattooed on the inside of his wrist, and an 'E' tattooed on the inside of his other wrist for Emma. Andy was a very hands on father, and a wonderful husband, just liked he vowed to be on our wedding day. I truly was a lucky woman.

Turning back to the stove, I scooped Hannah's scrambled eggs onto a plate so they could cool. While I finished up with our breakfast, the buzzer rang from downstairs.

"Baby, can you get the door?" I asked. Our out of town guests were right on time.

It was part of Andy's surprise. I heard him say "hello" over the intercom, and a second later, I heard Tamati and Iria call out, *"Kia ora."*

"Hey, come on up!" Andy said excitedly over the intercom as he buzzed them in. He jogged with Hannah back to the kitchen, kissed me on the cheek, and thanked me for his surprise visit from our friends.

He opened the front door and headed out with Hannah to meet them.

Iria and Tamati were finally able to come for a visit. After we left New Zealand, Iria had gotten pregnant, so they wanted to wait until after their baby was born and old enough to travel with them.

Their little boy, Jai, was ten months old. They had arrived the previous day and stayed at a hotel for the night, but they would stay with us the rest of the time they would be in Sacramento.

Andy had no idea they were coming.

A few minutes later, the group walked into the kitchen, the guys wheeling suitcases, and Iria, carrying a child on each hip. I hugged our friends, and held my arms out to Jai, so I could finally meet him in person. We had been keeping in close contact with them over Skype, so the kids were very familiar with each other. It was so cute when they visited over the computer screens, even though they spent most of their time trying to touch each other's hands on the screen.

Hannah knew Iria and Tamati as well. Jai came to me without hesitation, and Hannah stayed snuggled up with Iria. Jai had the biggest brown eyes and longest eyelashes I had ever seen. He was adorable with his dark, curly hair.

"You made it just in time for breakfast," I said to them. "I hope you're hungry."

Andy pulled plates and cups out of the cupboards and set the table for us, while Jai and I pulled a bowl of fresh fruit, milk and juice from the fridge, and handed them off to Tamati to take to the table.

I settled Jai in Hannah's highchair then fixed him a plate of scrambled eggs and tiny chunks of fruit. We sat at the table with our friends and caught up with each other over breakfast.

Later that morning, Andy and Tamati took the kids to the courtyard to play, while I helped Iria unpack in the guest room.

"Here are those items you wanted from En Zed, Zoey," Iria said slyly as she pulled a plastic bag from the large, inside pocket of her suitcase.

"Oh, thank you, thank you!" I clapped with excitement and accepted the bag from her. I sat on the bed and separated the things I'd asked her to bring me for Andy from the new clothes she'd brought for Hannah. I put the things for Andy into a gift bag then hid it in the closet until his surprise party this evening.

Later in the afternoon, Andy finally figured out what I was up to when everyone started showing up to the loft with food and gifts. Although the entire family came for the surprise party and barbecue, we kept it simple, burgers, and hot dogs, with several side dishes. And chocolate cake with chocolate frosting.

As I was frosting his cake, Andy snuck up behind me and slipped his arms around me, kissing my neck. He rubbed his palms across the lowest part of my flat stomach. Something he hadn't stopped doing, even after Hannah was born and I had lost the baby weight.

"Hi, my love, how has your thirty-first birthday been so far?"

"Best birthday ever, Zoey," he replied. "Thank you for everything." He was eyeing the cake in front of me.

I dipped my finger in the leftover frosting, and held it up to him. Sucking my finger into his mouth, he swirled his tongue around it, leaving not a trace of frosting.

He gave me *that* look, picked up the frosting container, put the lid on it, and stuck it in the fridge. "I'm saving that for tonight after everyone leaves," he whispered in my ear.

Hell yes!

Later, after everyone finished dinner, we had cake and homemade strawberry ice cream. I looked around at all our wonderful friends and family.

Adam and Angie had been married in May. Noah and Jess had their little girl, who they named Chloe. She was almost exactly the same age as Jai. Will and Justin had adopted an adorable four-year-old boy named Daniel.

Heather and Jason were here with Jake, Alex, and Mya. They were expecting baby number four in about three months. A couple months after the fire at the shop, Tara started dating Kyle Sherman. They were recently engaged, and I considered Tara a very dear friend of mine.

"Earth to Zoey!" Sasha bellowed from across the table.

I looked over at her and laughed.

She was sitting on Ben's knee and waving at me like she was trying to help land a 747 airplane. "Why the fuck didn't you tell me I should not be this fucking pregnant in August? I think I'm going to die of a heatstroke or drown in my own sweat."

I shrugged my shoulders. "Sorry, Sash. I'll remember next time."

She rolled her eyes at me.

She and Ben were also engaged, and planned to marry as soon as their baby was born.

As I continued to look around, I wondered where Jeremy was. I hadn't seen him in a while. My mom and dad sat under a large umbrella with Sarah and Hamish, sharing a bottle of wine from the case that they brought from Sonoma.

It was time for Andy to open his presents. He opened gifts from all our guests, and it was finally time to open my special gift to him.

I had hid the present at my feet under the table so it would be the last one he would open. I took Hannah off my lap, set her carefully on her feet, handed her the bag, and asked her to give it to her daddy.

She walked over and held it up to him. "Daddy pressie," she said in her tiny voice as she grinned up at him.

"Thank you, Hannah-banana." He smiled, using the same nickname he had given his sister when she was a small child.

He sat her on his lap, kissed her on the cheek then wrapped one arm safely around her while he opened the bag. He pulled out the tissue paper and then the stack of tiny black clothing.

I could tell by his expression that he recognized what he held in his hand.

He laid it on the picnic table then unfolded the tiny All Blacks onesie. In silver lettering across the front, it read,

I've been inside for 9 months, now let's play rugby.

He smiled over at me and his questioning eyes became watery.

"Zoey, are you trying to tell me what I *think* you're trying to tell me?"

I went and sat on his other knee across from Hannah. As our friends and family sat around us, clapping and congratulating us, I placed his free hand on my stomach where our second child was growing.

I leaned in and whispered in his ear, "Yes."

The End

Author Bio

Jen Andrews was raised in a small town in Northern California, and still lives in the same county where she was born. She is a self-proclaimed music and lyric addict. She grew up in a 'car family' so her life has been spent around old hot rods. She and her husband, Jake, even have a few of their own. In her spare time, Jen loves to travel wherever she can. She finally lived her dream of traveling to New Zealand to see her favorite rugby team, the All Blacks, play. Jen loves to do photography as a hobby and continues to write.

Find Jen here:

https://www.goodreads.com/author/show/7762025.Jen_Andrews

https://www.facebook.com/AuthorJenAndrews

https://www.facebook.com/jenandrewsauthor

https://www.goodreads.com/book/show/20755729-the-reason

https://www.goodreads.com/book/show/22585630-just-say-yes

https://www.goodreads.com/book/show/24312326-beautiful-with-you

https://twitter.com/jennysnowflakes

www.ingramcontent.com/pod-product-compliance
Lightning Source LLC
Chambersburg PA
CBHW032211190626
46810CB00019B/2488